THE
FORBIDDEN LIFE
OF
ALEX MOORE

A Beyond Novella

ERIN QUINN

THE FORBIDDEN LIFE OF ALEX MOORE
by Erin Quinn
Copyright © 2014 Erin Grady

Material excerpted from *The Three Fates of Ryan Love*
Copyright © 2015 by Erin Grady

ISBN: 978-0-9908876-0-7

To Liza Burns,
the little angel who has kept me sane this year.

CHAPTER ONE

OBVIOUSLY, THE WOMAN had no idea she was in danger. But she would. And soon, if Alex had the situation sized up right.

He'd been on a parallel course with her for the last ten minutes. She and four dogs traveled down an isolated trail that snaked the mountain from its peak to the pitted road below. She trudged, head lowered, her focus elsewhere. No more than a hundred paces away, Alex and Caleb moved through the trees like shadows. Alex was aware of every icy crystal that blustered in the wind, but the woman hadn't even noticed either of the men. Fortunately, neither had the dogs.

Alex glanced at the bloated sky pressing between the towering pines. It rode low to the ground, spewing fat snowflakes that stuck where they landed. What was the woman doing up here so close to dusk? With a blizzard chasing the encroaching dark? *Alone?*

And why did he care?

He wasn't here to protect humans. He was here for the hellhounds. His number had been called to protect the secrets of the Beyond, and he'd come to serve.

Assuming, of course, he could find the cursed creatures.

"Not very smart, is she?" Caleb muttered, drawing Alex's attention. The cold made a plume of his breath as he spoke.

Alex didn't like that Caleb watched the woman, too. And he didn't like that he didn't like it. He and Caleb were friends, yet they were bound by laws of the Beyond. No humans could be allowed to witness their mission. No exceptions.

"No," he answered grimly.

She'd stumbled into a situation she probably wouldn't survive. Most humans couldn't see the hellhounds or hear their disturbing howls. Most, but not all. If she was one of the rare few who could recognize them she'd have the advantage of knowing what came after her, but even if she avoided being eaten, she'd still have to die, by his hand or Caleb's.

Alex knew the rules. What soldier didn't? But he didn't like to think of this innocent female dying under either circumstance.

He watched her in bursts of color through the trees. Swatches of blue and pink and flashes of golden hair. He guessed her to be in her mid-twenties. Dressed in a puffy parka and polka-dotted cap with a yarn ball on top that bobbed as she walked, she looked like some sweet treat that would melt in the mouth.

Except for the rifle she carried. But that might be just for show. Odds were good that she didn't even know how to use it. She certainly didn't look like any killer Alex had ever seen, and he'd seen more than a few.

She probably felt safe with her big dogs and the gun.

"I can't believe they haven't picked her off already," Caleb said, mystified.

Alex couldn't believe it, either. He wanted to shake her, tell her to pay attention.

A loud crack came from a snow-laden branch of a nearby tree, and at last, her head came up. She slowed, wiped her eyes, and focused on her surroundings. Had she been crying?

Why do you care?

Alex knew the moment she spotted him among the trees. She froze for an instant, then glanced away, her chest rising and falling with agitated breaths. She quickly started walking again, this time with purpose. Good. Maybe she'd get out of here, away from the coming danger before it was too late. He let out a low sigh of relief, but at the same moment, the dogs caught sight of him and Caleb, and they started barking, raising an alarm that could probably be heard for miles.

"That'll do the trick," Caleb said under his breath.

In answer, a hellhound bayed a long, blood-chilling warning. They were coming.

The woman didn't know because she couldn't hear it, but the dogs did. All four stilled for a heartbeat before they renewed their barking with rabid fervor. One enormous dog with a square head and a booming bark bounded off in the direction of the sound. The other three weren't so big or eager to follow. They lagged behind, letting every predator on the mountain know where they were.

"Belle!" the woman called after the horse-dog, and then, before she could catch her breath, the other three decided to go after it.

"No!" she cried. "Come back!"

"Quiet," Alex whispered, feeling the wind shift. The icy blast carried the smell of sulfur on the air.

The woman's head whipped around as if she'd heard him, and she stared, wary. Her gaze shifted to Caleb in the background, then returned to Alex. Indecision flashed across her face before she straightened her spine and squared her shoulders. A human gesture, learned from nature: when in danger, try to look big.

It wouldn't help her.

She lifted her rifle, but she seemed too flustered to take aim. She glanced at the dogs disappearing up the trail, then back to the men who may or may not present a threat, then down at a small, furry thing at her feet that was begging to be picked up.

Another bay echoed from the forbidding peaks. Hungry and vicious.

"Here they come," Caleb said.

Alex didn't need the warning. He could feel the *chuff chuff* of their breaths, see the lathered hides, the gaping jaws.

He cut his eyes back to the woman. She was bent over a tiny dog, trying to catch it as it hopped anxiously around her legs. It looked like a prancing toy. Every time she got a hold on it, the stupid thing twisted away, yipping shrilly.

Alex didn't think—he didn't have time to think. He charged the woman in silence, hoping to scare her off without drawing the big dogs back. If he could get her to run, maybe he wouldn't have to watch her die. Or worse, kill her himself.

Behind him, he heard Caleb curse. "What the fuck are you doing?"

More chilling bays trilled through the twilight. Harsh. Bloody. *Close.*

She looked up, saw him coming toward her, and tried to maneuver the dog she'd finally captured and her rifle all at once. He reached her before she had the chance to shoot him, not that he thought she would. It took guts to pull the trigger on another human, and she had no reason to suspect he wasn't one.

He grabbed the barrel of her rifle and shoved it in the air. She pulled the trigger just as it cleared the top of his head. The blast burned his hand, rang in his ears, and told him he'd underestimated her. If he'd been a split second slower he'd be dead.

The rifle's kick pushed her back as he used his momentum to yank her forward. He caught her with his free arm, each of them gripping the rifle between them.

It brought her close enough to him that he could smell the clean scent of her shampoo, the warm fragrance of her skin, the sweet puff of her breath. The coat padded her figure, but beneath she felt small framed and lushly curved. Her breasts pressed against his chest, indescribably soft and weighted. She balanced on her toes and his hips found the cradle of hers, rousing feelings that lit his nerve endings and heated his blood. All the while her scent wrapped around his thoughts like an opiate, guiding him to a place he'd never want to leave.

She stared at him with wide, blue eyes flecked with crystals of white and lavender fringed by long, golden-tipped lashes. He'd never seen anything so beautiful, so arresting.

The hellhounds howled again, a litany of menace that tore him from the mesmerizing sensations.

"You need to run," he said hoarsely, his gaze still trapped by hers, her body against his. Now was the time to let her go, to push her away. But neither of them moved. In her arms, the little dog growled and snapped at him. Under other circumstances, Alex might have been amused. But right now, hellhounds were coming.

The deep, loud barks of her other dogs in the near distance stopped on an abrupt yelp. The woman's eyes widened in fear. At the same time, halfway down the slope to Alex's left, the trees shivered, as if something had brushed against them on its way to the bottom.

"Run," he said, desperate now as all hope of chasing her quietly out of danger dissolved. His arms finally opened. "Run, you deranged female."

She pushed away from him and the cold rushed into the space her warm body left behind. She shouted for her dogs as she bolted down the trail and into the deepening gloom. The dogs barked in excited response, and Alex heard them barreling down the trail after her.

Another wail whipped over the treetops and whisked around the mountain peaks. Instantly, an answer came, this one low and fierce, from the ridges to the south. More hellhounds joined in, baying a cold, hostile challenge. Alex pulled out his blade—an iron machete that weighed twice what it should—and spun around. He met Caleb's gaze across the distance that divided them.

They'd trained for this, yet nothing could have prepared them for the real thing. Like the human world itself, the intensity of the hellhounds bearing down on them was too strong to ever be simulated.

The first hellhound slipped out of shadow like the demon it was. Huge and hulking, it held its head low, white eyes glowing like lanterns in its black skull. Like a bizarre melding of what seemed to be several different creatures, it moved with all the grace of a lion but none of the beauty. The shoulders rolled, the head bobbed, and the teeth . . . So many teeth . . . And all shiny and sharp.

The woman's dogs had been fierce, but this creature was ferocious and frightening, covered in a leathery hide with sparse fur and tremendous jaws. Jaws that could easily crack bone and tear limbs from bodies.

The thought barely formed before another black blur streaked into sight, heading past him and after the retreating woman. The horse-sized dog bringing up the rear of her pack spun to search the chaos it had left behind, looking for . . . What? Surely it sensed that what came next would be slaughter?

It didn't matter now. Maybe the huge dog would at least delay the hellhound long enough for the woman to escape. Alex wished it so, but at this point, all he could do was stand between her and the other hellhounds . . . and just hope she would survive.

Both Alex and Caleb held their weapons at the ready. Hewn from the purest iron, treated with the salts of the Dead Sea and the power of the Beyond, these blades—and no others—could kill these heinous abominations. He sliced the air in front of him and bent his knees to take a powerful, sturdy stance. Twenty feet to his left, Caleb did the same. The hounds bayed relentlessly, but Alex tuned inward, focusing on the weight of his weapon, the goal of his mission. He'd counted six hellhounds total, including the one that had raced after the woman, but more could be lurking in the scrub and shadows. He and Caleb hadn't expected even half as many.

Three of the creatures paced in front of Alex, snapping and baring teeth that looked as thick and long as Alex's fingers. The beasts chortled a strange and eerie message to one another as they eyed his blade with aversion. Their snarls made his bones feel cold and his blood too thick to pump.

"Come on," he muttered, but the hellhounds didn't move. They seemed to be waiting for something.

On cue, a seventh hound stalked from the trees. The others watched it with hungry eyes, snouts dropped in

8

obeisance as it moved through their ranks with haughty disregard, not even bothering to glance their way. Still the other hounds shrank back. *The leader . . .*

Carefully, without a word spoken between them, Alex and Caleb drew closer together, knowing they'd need to work in tandem if they hoped to kill the beasts. The apparent leader watched with disdain. The message was clear: they could gang up, pool their power, and wield their weapons, but still they'd be nothing more than snacks with legs.

Alex gripped his machete more tightly, wondering if the woman had made it to shelter or if her bloody remains even now stained the earth. The thought disturbed him and disrupted his focus. He shouldn't care. Casualties were expected. But the thought of those beautiful eyes closed forever made his gut clench.

"How many more do you think there are?" Caleb asked as the beasts formed a circle around him and Alex.

"Five? Fifty?"

"That's my count, too." Caleb smiled grimly. "See you on the other side, brother."

A promise of comrades. Today they might die protecting the Beyond, but tomorrow they would awake in the afterlife, purified by their sacrifice.

Or so they'd been promised.

Alex and Caleb turned their backs to one another just as the first hellhound lunged. Others followed, countering every move Alex and Caleb made with the kind of military precision that proved they were capable of higher thinking, regardless of their feral appearance.

They flanked the men, launching synchronized assaults from all sides. A small, wiry beast hung back, watching and assessing, while the leader bounded up onto a boulder that gave it a bird's-eye view of the battle. It surveyed them with its eerie eyes, its teeth bared. Strategizing. Only a fool would see it as anything less.

Alex took it all in as he swung his blade, intent on cutting through the first hound he reached and clearing a direct path to the leader. But before he realized it, three of the creatures darted in with a skill he could hardly grasp, attacking and evading, managing to draw him away, isolating him from both Caleb and his goal. It appeared they'd done the same to his partner, who fought with a steady, if frantic, pace as more hounds widened the divide between the two men with strategic assaults. Vulnerable with his back exposed now, Alex stabbed at the lunging beasts but they moved too fast and he barely drew blood before they scurried away. Wearing him down. He recognized the tactic even as he felt himself tire.

The leader leaped from the boulder, fierce determination glinting in its eyes, intent on finishing him off. Alex feinted to the right, turning mid-step and catching the alpha in flight. Blood spewed from its wound, its body going one way, the head another. He finished his rotation, catching a different one with the machete and eviscerating it with a slice it didn't see coming.

Another creature sideswiped Alex with a body blow that took him to his knees. It was exactly the opportunity the small, wiry one had obviously been waiting for. The beast landed on top of Alex as he tried to roll away. Claws tore his coat and dug down into his flesh. One hellhound sank its teeth into his leg, another his opposite arm, keeping him pinned for the wiry one to annihilate.

Alex took a deep breath, knowing it might be his last. He'd imagined when he faced the threshold of the promised afterlife, he'd be light of spirit, ready to embrace it. Instead the memory of wide, blue eyes, crystalline and tinted with lavender flashed through his mind and something inside him clenched with the realization that he'd never know what thoughts filled those swirling depths.

Before he could follow that perplexing thought, the beast atop him cocked its head and scanned the distance. An instant later, a furious bout of barking joined the guttural growls and vicious howls of the hounds. From the corner of his eye, Alex saw a mottled blur speed across the patches of snow.

The woman's dog.

Dread pooled inside him. Surely the woman wouldn't have come back?

The dog plowed into the hellhound poised on top of Alex, knocking it off and following it down to the ground. New barks joined the chaos, and Alex's heart seized with fear.

The hounds still had him pinned down and another huge one pounced on top of him, moving in for the kill. Alex couldn't get his arm free, couldn't get the hilt of his machete in a grip that would allow him to swing with his other hand. He bucked and twisted, but it was no use.

A blast from behind him echoed off the shadowed mountains and snow-banked sky. Something massive collapsed on top of him, nearly crushing his chest. Another shot and the teeth in his thigh let loose as the hellhound yelped in pain.

Alex renewed his struggle, trying to get his sword free, trying to get out from under the weight that had him trapped. The hellhound that had gone for his throat lay prone on top of him, its skull ripped open. Same for the one sprawled beside him. Several shots sounded from behind him, and bullets tunneled into the hard ground, spraying dirt everywhere. One bullet caught an advancing hound in the flank. The creature snapped deadly jaws in Alex's direction as it backed away. Another shot caught a different hound in the gut, and the wounded beast bounded away, leaving a trail of blood behind. Alex finally managed to turn his head around to see where the gunfire was coming from.

The woman with the pink polka-dotted hat and puffy blue coat stood ten feet away, her rifle up and her pretty blue eyes staring at him down the barrel. Her dogs growled from beside her, their fur standing on end and eyes wild.

The woman had come back to help him. A stranger. He didn't understand why she'd done it, but the kindness of the act burrowed deep within him. He couldn't let her repayment be death by hellhound.

The big, mottled horse-dog—she'd called it Belle—and the wiry hellhound ran from the cover of the trees, side by side. Confused, Alex watched Belle spin to a stop in front of the woman. The dog gave a deep, commanding bark and the hellhound halted, too. The woman's other dogs shrank back, brushing against her legs to avoid contact with the hellhound, but Belle barked again, communicating something that calmed the others. Not even the little one ran, nor did the bigger ones turn on the abomination in their midst.

Gloriously fearless, Belle nudged the wiry hellhound with her snout, as if it were a collie instead of a killer of the most devious breed. The two animals were nearly the same size, but that didn't make them equal. Why didn't the hellhound attack? Kill?

Instead, it stood docilely beside Belle, its tongue lolling against its black gums, canines so long they curled as huge spires of saliva dripped down to the ground. It had massive jaws, a built-to-slaughter body, and it could rip the woman in two with minimal effort. But it didn't even try.

At last, Alex freed himself from the deadweight on top of him and stumbled to his feet. Blood soaked the earth, and slain hellhounds lay scattered all around him. His gaze found Caleb, mangled and unmoving on the ground not far away. His eyes stared sightlessly upward. His throat had been ripped open, and the hounds had feasted on him until there was no hope that he'd ever draw breath again.

Pain seared Alex from the inside out. They'd been friends, of a sort. As close as any creature of the Beyond was allowed to be. He turned away with a heavy heart and hefted his blade in preparation for whatever came next. His thigh burned from deep bites, his chewed arm dripping blood.

The woman watched him with equal parts fear and concern. The wiry hellhound still stood near her. Why did it look like it had joined her pack in protecting her? What were the other surrounding hellhounds waiting for? Why didn't they attack? And what was with her crazy dog?

The woman looked as though she had as many questions as he did. Her eyes shifted from side to side, scanning for danger. He met her confused gaze and saw the panic lurking there.

"Back away," he said softly.

She remained frozen in place. She was afraid to move and she couldn't even see the hellhounds. She'd been shooting blind, aiming at the symptom without seeing the disease. She didn't know that one of the creatures stood at her feet.

As if hearing his thoughts, the hellhound gave a deep, threatening growl that rumbled low in its throat. The other hellhounds skittered back—just a step. Just enough to betray their fear.

Bewildered, Alex watched the creature stare down the others, only then noticing its eyes. Hellhounds had eyes like the winter moon—silver-white moons that glowed with blood thirst—but this one's eyes were icy blue, so pale he might have missed the coloring if the beast hadn't been standing still.

The moment stretched as Alex braced for the violence threatening to erupt. The woman cocked her rifle just as the blue-eyed hellhound lunged at Alex. He was ready to cut it down, but it veered and brushed passed him with only a glance as it launched itself at its brethren, chasing them into the woods.

"Belle, stay!" the woman said sharply, calling her dog back when she tried to follow.

Alex watched with shock as the creatures disappeared into the forest, leaving him standing in a clearing filled with dead hellhounds, owing his life to a human female—one dressed up like a blue-frosted cupcake with pink sprinkles on top.

CHAPTER TWO

LILLY WASN'T GOING to shoot the stranger, but she didn't lower the barrel of the rifle, either. She wasn't going to do anything that might bring back . . .

"What the hell was that?" she demanded, still trying to find words for what she'd seen. Rather, what she *hadn't* seen.

The man standing in front of her looked ready to keel over, but he managed to catch her gaze and hold it with his strangely colored eyes. Not brown, not green, but some mixed-up, striking version of both. He looked nearly as stunned as she felt.

She squared her shoulders and scowled when he didn't answer. "I asked you a question."

"I can't answer you," he said.

"You can or I'll call 9-1-1 and tell them there's been a shooting. Possibly a fatal one."

Her words made him pause. Not that he believed her. She wouldn't have believed her, either. She was shaking so hard she had to give in and lower the barrel of her rifle. Her dogs circled anxiously at her feet. Harley—a petite Pomeranian who thought he was king of the jungle—danced on his hind legs and rested his front paws on her knees. His fluffy little ears were pinned and his brown eyes wide. Poor thing was terrified. So was she.

"Is that a dog?" the stranger asked in a deep, husky voice. He stared at Harley with both fascination and disgust.

Lilly scooped up the little dog. "What were *they*?" she repeated. It was hard to look tough with a Pomeranian in your arms, but she did her best.

"They?"

She nodded. It had felt like *they*. Many. Multiple. An invisible threat that had come from all sides. Whatever *they* were, they'd left tracks and blood. They'd held the stranger down. At least that's how it had seemed. She'd fired at them, not even knowing what she was shooting.

The man gave her a hard look and she thought he might not answer again. It seemed to worry him, her asking about them. It worried her, too.

"Tell me," she said, and fear gave the order a ring of desperation he undoubtedly heard.

"Hellhounds," he answered in a low voice.

"What?"

"You heard me. And standing around talking about it won't change anything."

Surely, she'd heard wrong. She swept the clearing with her disbelieving gaze, remembering the sense of danger so thick it had nearly paralyzed her. When the stranger had told her to run, she had. She'd *felt* the peril in the air. But Belle had bounded back toward the man

17

and Lilly had gone after her. She'd seen the Great Dane slam into something, even though she couldn't see what that something was. And it seemed to be holding the man down as he flailed. Then she'd watched in horror while his limbs had been jerked and torn at by something that churned the dirt and gravel.

It had been terrifying and confusing. Even now, she couldn't put a framework around her memories. But *hellhounds?* Was he crazy? Was she?

"Why couldn't I see them?"

"Because you're human. You're not meant to see them."

"Because I'm human?" she repeated. She managed to nail the calm tone but couldn't stop her shaking in her hands.

He didn't answer. She hadn't expected him to.

Lilly brought her gun back up when he moved forward, though. His unsteady legs might have undermined his arrogant manner, but that didn't make him less menacing.

He brushed her weapon out of the way and stared down at her. He was so tall she had to look up to meet his gaze. Beneath his black jacket, muscle layered his arms and shoulders, his powerful chest. She'd had a taste of his strength when he'd yanked the barrel of her rifle up and held her against him. If he'd wanted to hurt her, he could have done it then in less time than it had taken him to whisper, *Run.* The thought helped to quiet her fear.

"Who are you?" she asked.

"Alex Moore."

He offered his name like it should mean something. Anything.

"Why are you here?"

"Why are you?"

Lilly scowled. "That's none of your business."

"My reason's not yours, either."

He raised his brows, daring her to argue. She might have been intimidated if not for the way his hand trembled where it gripped the hilt of a blade that stopped just short of being a sword.

A machete. That's what it was. The man was carrying a freaking *machete.* He took another step closer.

"That's close enough," she told him.

With a shake of his head, he sheathed his weapon and raised his bloody hands, palms out. "I mean you no harm."

His deep voice carried a reassuring tone. The kind that could lull a girl into misplaced trust if she wasn't careful.

She wanted to believe him, though. She was up here, miles from the nearest city, all alone with nothing but an empty shotgun and a pack of dogs she'd inherited from her sister. Of course she wanted to believe he meant her no harm.

His unusual eyes were the only light in a face that didn't smile. He was big, covered in gore, and out in the middle of nowhere. Her gaze shifted to the mutilated body of the man who'd been with him. She'd arrived in time to see something eviscerate him, but all she'd witnessed was his thrashing and screaming and a bloody death that seemed to be inflicted by the churning air around him.

The stranger—Alex Moore—watched her with a guarded expression. His eyes shimmered with pain.

"Was he your friend?" she asked softly.

"Yes."

The word rounded the sharp edge of emotion, emerging a little rough, a little weary. Lilly understood. Her sister had died less than a month ago and the loss still felt like an echo chamber. Hollow but for her grief and memories.

"I'm sorry," she said.

He looked startled by the sentiment, or maybe it was the empathy he heard in her voice. For a moment, their eyes locked again. He had truly beautiful eyes.

Face hot, she glanced away while she fumbled for her phone in her pocket. Getting a signal would be a miracle, though. It was iffy up here on a clear day. Today the clouds made a thick, seemingly impenetrable, barrier.

"What are you doing?" he asked when she held her phone in the air and turned.

"Looking for a signal. You need a doctor and your friend . . ."

Needs a coroner.

"No. We need to get out of here before they come back."

20

She agreed wholeheartedly. The sense of eminent threat may have faded with the stench of rotten eggs, but she didn't doubt for a moment that it—*they*—would return. Of course they would, those ghostly demons that could rip a man to pieces without being seen.

She cast a troubled gaze at the woods and then back to Alex.

"What about your friend?" she asked gently.

"He's gone."

"I know, but . . . you don't want to just leave him here, do you?"

He gave her a flat look. "Yes."

Eyes wide, she watched as he unsheathed his machete. Graceful. Fast. Cirque du Soleil . . . with hellhounds.

He walked through the blood-soaked clearing, paused, and drove his blade down to the ground.

"What are you doing?" she asked.

"Making sure they're dead."

Which meant *they* were still there, lying in bloody pools a few feet away. He pulled his machete free before bracing and bringing it down again in a chopping motion.

"What are you doing now?"

He gave her a dark look. "Making sure they stay dead."

Oh.

"You shot three of them," he said in a casual tone as he moved to the next crimson puddle.

"I did?"

He nodded. "Head shots on two of them." He slid a curious glance her way. "How did you do that?"

"I'm a good shot."

"But you couldn't see them."

"I could see you."

His narrowing eyes met hers. She hadn't intended that to sound so deep, but it had. And now she felt as though being the first one to look away would give it more meaning.

Interminable seconds ticked by before Alex broke the connection and went back to swinging his machete. Relieved, Lilly swallowed hard and glanced at the dogs near her feet. She heard a *thunk* and turned to see Alex's blade resisting his attempt to pull it free. He had to put his foot down on whatever the machete was stuck in to tug it loose. Lilly's stomach roiled at the sight.

"Not even a hellhound can come back from that," he told her, clearly satisfied with himself.

"Good job?" she offered.

He gave a curt nod. *You're welcome.*

Methodically, he worked through the bodies of the hellhounds only he could see. Stabbing, severing. Sometimes he had to kick and hack. At Lilly's feet, her sister's dogs watched with curious eyes. All but Belle. She paced with agitation. Lilly gave her an uneasy look, wishing she understood the animals better—or at all.

"Let's go," Alex said at last, cleaning his bloody knife with snow before wiping it against his jean-clad leg and sheathing it.

"Where?" she asked, startled.

He walked right up to her without even *one* of the dogs making a move to stop him, took her arm, and turned her around the way she'd come.

"This way," he said.

Well, that made everything clearer.

Harley growled in her arms and showed his little teeth.

"Quiet," Alex ordered.

Harley shut up but made sure to flash his canines whenever Alex looked his way. Alex kept hold of her arm and set a brisk pace back to the trail, back to her Range Rover, through a world of falling snow and isolation. Only a fool would go with him.

"You're no safer out here," he muttered when she hesitated.

She glanced over her shoulder. The other four dogs trotted behind her. Even Belle, but she paused to look back with a wistful whine.

"I can keep up without you dragging me along," Lilly informed him a few steps later.

He looked at his long fingers wrapped around the sleeve of her parka and reluctantly let go.

"Don't slow down," he warned.

No *or else* followed, but Lilly didn't need it. She made sure she didn't fall behind. If the hellhounds came back, she wouldn't stand a chance against them alone. Her gun was empty, the dogs unpredictable, and she couldn't even see the things. He, at least, had a weapon and knew what he fought.

She couldn't even form a mental image of what a hellhound might look like. All she got when she tried was red eyes and big teeth. She didn't want to know if she was close, either.

Hellhounds.

Did she really believe that's what had attacked him and his friend?

She kept walking, remembering the blood, the violence that hung in the air, the fear. . . .

Yeah, evidently she did.

She pulled in a shaking breath and stared straight ahead. Not at the tall man beside her. Not over her shoulder, either, where he'd left his mutilated friend.

Jesus. That just happened.

"How did you know what they were?" she asked between pants as she kept pace.

"What are you doing out here all alone?" he countered instead of answering.

"Looking for my dog. She ran off."

"Try a leash next time."

She shot him a dirty look. She would *love* to try a leash. But taking five dogs out on leashes was a death-defying act way above her skill set.

"I wasn't walking them when it happened," Lilly said. "Belle jumped the fence in my backyard a few nights ago. When I couldn't find her, I came here."

"Why here?"

Lilly debated the wisdom of answering. Belle had come *here* because this was an area the dog knew. Lilly's sister, Amy, had lived in a cabin not far away.

Home, as far as Belle was concerned. But did she want this stranger to know that?

Lilly settled on an edited version of the truth. "They're my sister's dogs. She rescued and trained them. I don't know what to do with them. I don't speak dog."

The corners of his mouth kicked up.

"Where's your sister?"

So much for circumventing that conversation.

"She died. A few weeks ago." Lilly paused and took a deep breath, hoping it would calm the welling emotions. "Belle took it hard."

Those four words said way more than she'd intended. Tears blurred her vision and her voice wobbled. She blinked back the tears but Alex's gaze lingered on her eyes, noting the pain there.

"That's why you were crying earlier," he said. "Before the attack."

She nodded, wondering how long he'd been watching her without her knowing it. She took another deep breath and went on.

"Belle started acting funny when I was packing to take them home—to my home. I thought she'd get over it once we got there. I didn't know . . . I never had a dog until I had five." Her laugh sounded weak. She cut it off quickly. "I didn't know what I didn't know."

Alex stopped walking. Lilly kept going, hoping to avoid whatever was coming, but Alex didn't budge and reluctantly, she stopped, too. He made an irritated sound and came to stand in front of her, closer than she'd expected. She didn't look up, though. Not even when he brushed a tear away with fingers warm from his pockets.

"What are you called?" he asked.

She chanced a glance at his face. "Other than *deranged female?*"

His eyes crinkled at the corners and amusement gleamed in their coppery depths. She tried not to stare, but even a hint of a smile changed his features, making him look younger, more approachable.

That didn't make him any less dangerous, but Lilly couldn't help but let her guard slip a little more.

"My name's Lilly Winslow."

"Lilly," he said, testing the sound in that deep voice of his. Making her feel it in places she shouldn't. "Like your eyes."

He'd noticed her eyes? Disconcerted, she corrected his mistake. "Lilacs and lavender are purple and blue. Lilies are white."

He thought for a moment before nodding. "Lavender," he said softly.

There was no reason for it, but the murmured word felt intimate. It made her agitated and achy. The way he said it, the way he gazed at her as he spoke.

"This trail leads to your sister's place?" he asked, switching subjects so smoothly she felt immediately distrustful again.

"Why do you want to know that?"

"Relax, Lilly. I'm just trying to figure out why your dog came *here.*"

Oh. That made sense. He must've thought it had to do with the hellhounds, but the reason was much simpler.

"This was Amy's favorite trail. Up at the top, there's a view that makes you feel like you're in heaven."

His eyes widened with surprise. She didn't understand the reaction, but he didn't give her time to question it.

"What was the dog doing when you found her?" Alex asked.

Lilly shrugged. "Coming back down."

His brow furrowed in the silence that followed. She knew he was remembering how Belle had charged into the woods. Had she been chasing off the hellhounds? Would the big dog take on a creature that could kill a grown man—an *armed* grown man—in a matter of seconds?

"Where are you from?" she blurted.

"I wouldn't be doing you any favors by answering that," he said. "I've already told you too much."

"How did the hellhounds get here?" she tried again anyway.

"Why did you come back to help me?" he shot back.

"I didn't. I was chasing my dog."

"You didn't have to stop."

"Quit deflecting. Why are there hellhounds in these mountains?"

"It's forbidden for me to tell you. It's forbidden for me to know."

"It's a little late to worry about that now. I just shot three of them."

He exhaled heavily, giving a reluctant nod of concession. "They were left behind."

"By?"

"By someone who shouldn't have been here in the first place. Your world and mine . . . they aren't so different. They both have good guys and bad guys."

Her mouth was dry, her throat constricted. "What do you mean, your world and my world?"

"Does your world have hellhounds?"

"No."

"That's what I mean."

Lilly frowned. He didn't look insane, but did he really think she'd buy this story? He thought they came from different *worlds*. She should be laughing . . . or running. Or both.

Instead, she asked, "So where the hell *is* your world?"

He didn't answer, and the hard set of his jaw told her she wouldn't get any more out of him. Because he hadn't made up that part yet?

Cautiously, Lilly came at it from a different angle. "You can travel back and forth between our worlds?"

The look he slid her way was definitely annoyed. "You ask too many questions."

"Can you?"

"For limited periods of time."

"Like a weekend pass?"

"That would imply I want to go where they send me."

"You didn't want to come here?"

"No."

"Why not?" she asked.

"It's never as nice as the brochure."

She let that settle in to her bewilderment. He hadn't wanted to come here, and he'd been sent. From another world. To hunt hellhounds. With a *machete*. *Hellhounds.* Something humans weren't meant to see but he could. So what did that make him? Alien? Demon? Delusional?

She took a deep, frozen breath. "What about the ones that got away?"

"I'll find them. Eventually."

"And then you'll go home? Back to your world?"

He gave her another sideways look that did the talking for him.

Right. If he told her, he'd have to kill her. Best thing she could do right now was shut up and run. Fear made her calculate how fast she could get away, but fear also kept her by his side. She was screwed either way.

"Should I be afraid of you?" she asked.

He stopped and turned so suddenly she plowed right into him. He steadied her as he stared into her eyes. His glimmered with something she couldn't define, but he touched her face again, as if he couldn't help himself. His hand warm against her cold cheek, he leaned in.

"Yes," he said, his breath a hot burst against her temple. "You should be afraid."

29

But fear wasn't the emotion those words inspired. Lilly thought it might be a good time to breathe, but she couldn't seem to do it until he stepped away. She had more questions—of course she did. But she kept them inside as they trudged along in silence. Her boots were loud against the frozen dirt and grit. Her heartbeat was even louder in her ears.

Alex kept an unrelenting pace, but the limp on his right side had become more pronounced. She remembered watching that leg being jerked, as though something big had a hold on it. Her gaze moved to his arm. The sleeve of his coat gleamed with a wet sheen. It looked like blood. How badly was he hurt?

She didn't ask that, either. Her silence seemed to trouble him, though. She intersected several heavy-lidded glances but she couldn't tell what he might be thinking. Maybe he was wondering how to ditch her, and then she wouldn't have to worry about running away before she led him right to her sister's isolated cabin.

"Humans can't handle a truth like hellhounds," he said as if she'd been peppering him with questions and finally wormed the answer out of him. "You should think they're a myth, not have to gun them down to stay alive."

She'd let him get away without explaining it the first he'd said *humans* as if he wasn't one of them. She didn't intend to let it happen again.

"So you're from another world and you're not human," she said like she wasn't completely freaked out.

He shot her a guarded glance but didn't respond.

"You look human," she said.

"It's intended."

Something deep moved through those words, something she couldn't begin to guess at, but she felt the confusion and frustration behind them. She wanted to pry, make him tell her what it meant, all that churning feeling she heard in his voice.

"But just to be clear, you're not human? That's what you're saying, isn't it?"

He'd been looking ahead, scanning the gloom-filled trail. Now he turned his beautiful, unusual eyes on Lilly. They made her feel unsettled, like a leaf caught in a riptide.

He walked with shoulders raised against the cold, his arms held against his body. He looked like the man next door. He looked like the man you'd never get close enough to know, no matter how hard you tried. A gust blew his dark hair across his forehead and tugged at the fleece of his jacket, but he didn't look away. Lilly couldn't, either.

"Yes," he said at last. "That's what I'm saying."

His voice was tight. She'd forced a confession he hadn't wanted to make. And yet, beneath his ire, she heard regret that settled around them like the silent snow. All Lilly knew about him was that he carried a big knife, had eyes like pennies at the bottom of a well, and didn't think he was human. No common ground existed between them. Yet, in that moment, she felt as if they shared more than a bloody patch of snow and unanswerable questions.

Whoever he was, he didn't intend to hurt her, but he didn't belong here. Like the hellhounds she couldn't see, Alex was from a different place. One he was forbidden to discuss with humans. One Lilly knew must be fraught with danger. A smart woman would take her dogs and run, and Lilly had always considered herself smarter than most.

But when Alex said, "We need to move faster," Lilly didn't counter with, *Why don't we go our separate ways?*

Instead, she picked up her pace.

CHAPTER THREE

THEY WERE NEAR the bottom of the trail. In her mind, Lilly could see the bend up ahead and the sharp slope that led down to the road. She'd left her Range Rover—*Amy's* Range Rover. Lilly drove an economical Prius when she wasn't carpooling with five dogs—tucked up behind the giant boulder that marked the turnoff to the cabin.

Evening shadows had grown impossibly long, and the sun hovered, awaiting its last moment before falling behind the western ridges. Grainy dusk rushed out from the horizon and dropped into the canyons and gullies. The trees became dark giants and the cold, an enemy.

Anxiously, Lilly watched the snow coming down. Thick and steady, it blustered around them, faster now than it had been, making her cheeks sting. Her feet were frozen, her skin numb. She was glad they'd reach the SUV soon, but she still didn't know what she'd do when they got there.

Alex's limp was worse, too, and his shoulder brushed against hers as he took each obviously painful step. Through the layers of coats and cold, she felt a spark that raced over her flesh and settled somewhere low and deep. How did he do that to her? Was it some otherworldly superpower?

The way down to the road below was steep and rocky. Alex stepped on a slippery patch and lurched hard to the right. Lilly quickly reached out to steady him, putting his arm over her shoulder and her arm around his waist. Even through his fleece coat, she could feel steel bands of hard muscle. She might provide a bit of balance, but if he went down, she was going with him.

"How bad are you hurt, Alex?"

"I'm not hurt."

"Then why are you limping?"

He immediately shifted away from her and stumbled to his knees. As predicted, she went down with him, his muffled groan in her ear, his weight pinning her to the ground.

"Sorry," he muttered, trying to extricate himself, but he was pale and shaky.

Lilly managed to get to her feet, but when she reached to help him up, she found the sleeves of his coat stiff and sticky with blood. How much had he lost? She took his face between her hands, the feel of his skin a shock to her system. His cheeks were ice cold.

"Alex, look at me."

He raised his bleary eyes and focused on her face, but it seemed an effort.

"Where'd you learn to shoot a rifle like that?" he asked, slurring his words.

"YouTube. Alex, where else are you hurt? Your leg and . . . ?"

"Arm. Shoulder." He paused to wince. "Fucker took a chunk out of my ribs."

Lilly cursed softly, looking around as if for an answer. In the distance, a wolf gave a long, mournful serenade. At least she thought it was a wolf. And it *sounded* far away, but what if it wasn't?

"We need to get inside," Alex said, the words thick and slow. "Shelter."

"You think?"

She moved behind him and heaved against his body, helping him to his feet and then ducking under his arm again to get a grip on him. The dogs raced ahead as she and Alex navigated the hazardous slope to the dirt road and her vehicle, parked just where she'd left it. Thank God.

His bulk, gravity, balance—it all seemed to be working against them. Stubbornly, he tried to shrug off her support.

She shot him an aggravated look. "Are you afraid I'll think you're a sissy if you lean on me?"

Arrogance gleamed in his amused gaze. "I'm not afraid of anything."

"Spoken like a man."

"Not a man, either."

There was no missing the anger in *those* words. Nor could she miss the disappointment that lodged somewhere beneath her breastbone. For reasons she

35

didn't want to analyze, his previous denials of humanity hadn't bothered her nearly as much as those four words.

"Are you also immune to pain?" she asked sweetly.

He hesitated before letting loose a soft, annoyed sigh. He shook his head.

"I didn't think so."

When they reached the SUV, he leaned against the side while Lilly opened the hatch for the dogs. Dutifully, they jumped in and made themselves comfortable on their blankets. Even Belle, though she had to be asked twice. Harley waited to be lifted like the royalty he thought himself to be. She closed them in and moved to stand in front of Alex.

His face was white, his lips tinged blue, and sweat beaded his brow. He scanned the gloaming with such worried eyes that his tension coiled around her.

"What's going on, Alex? Do you hear something?"

He considered his answer. She could almost see him moving the words around in his head as he searched for the right order.

"Bad things," he said at last, his voice gruff, low. "They're coming."

"I'd say they're already here."

He shook his head. "Not yet."

"You mean things worse than hellhounds?"

She hadn't said it loudly, but the cold seemed to ride her question, making it whip around them. She felt the echo, the frosty bite of fear. The sound of a stone bouncing down a rock-strewn hill made them both turn to look into the textured darkness. It had gathered into a tight cocoon over the landscape.

"Got any bullets left in that rifle?" he asked.

She shook her head. "There's some in the glove box, though."

He narrowed his eyes at something she couldn't see. "You won't make it."

He'd said it so softly, she thought she'd misheard until a man stepped out of the trees. For a second, she was relieved. A man she could see had to be better than hellhounds she couldn't. But then she noticed the machete he gripped in his hands. And he didn't lower it when he saw them.

"Do you know this guy?" she whispered.

Alex nodded, but he clearly wasn't glad to see the newcomer. He straightened, hiding his weakness and injuries with a stiff spine. He didn't reach for his weapon, but she'd seen how quickly he could draw it. In the chilled silence, he watched the man approach. There may have been recognition in his expression, but Lilly saw no welcome.

"Where is Caleb?" the stranger demanded.

"Dead," Alex answered.

The stranger cut his eyes to Lilly. In the SUV, her sister's five dogs barked fiercely and frantically, clawing at the glass and making it muddy with dirt and saliva. Could she get back to open the hatch before this stranger . . . What? Chopped her in half with his machete? Is that what she expected him to do? For all she felt inexplicably safe with Alex, this new man . . . not so much.

"Thank you for aiding my friend," he said in a kindly voice.

Beside her, Alex stiffened, as if a threat had come hidden inside the hollow words of gratitude.

"Anyone would have helped him," she answered cautiously.

"You weren't afraid?" the stranger asked.

Lilly glanced at Alex's drawn face, trying to read the undercurrents of the conversation. But Alex didn't look at her and his expression gave nothing away.

"Of course I was afraid. Only a fool wouldn't be."

That seemed to amuse the other man. "I imagine you saw things that you thought only lived in nightmares," he went on.

She kept her breath steady, but her pulse hammered out of control. Hidden mines lay waiting in this innocuous exchange. Like the hellhounds, she could feel them, even if she couldn't see them.

"What do you mean?"

The question startled him, and she felt Alex's apprehension escalate. She hoped her expression looked as emotionless as his, but beneath the surface, panic ricocheted inside her. Alex shifted his weight away from her and, so calmly she almost didn't realize what he was doing, he positioned himself slightly in front of her.

"Does she know the consequences of helping you?" the stranger asked Alex, his concern empty in the frosted twilight.

"She found me after it went down, Jared," Alex answered evenly. "There will be no consequences. She saw nothing. She did nothing wrong."

"But she will," the stranger said.

The certainty in his voice stroked Lilly's fear and trembled through her limbs. What consequences? What wrong did they expect her to do? It took everything not to blurt out the questions, but Lilly sensed that anything she said would be dangerous. Alex had told her humans weren't meant to know about hellhounds. Lilly was smart enough to guess he'd understated the situation.

"She *will* talk, Alex," Jared said. "She's human. She won't be able to help herself."

Denying that she had anything to talk about seemed pointless. This man had made up his mind. Everything in his tone, his demeanor, his expression told her that. But not saying anything implied guilt.

"Finding an injured man and helping him is hardly breaking news," she said.

Jared smiled. "But that's not all you found, is it?"

She should have stuck with the guilty silence.

"Have you ever heard of Abaddon?" Jared asked.

"No."

"But you're familiar with hell?"

She crossed her arms. "I might have heard of that one."

"And the devil? You know him?"

Her mouth was dry and her fingers shook, but she forced herself to keep her cool. "Not personally."

He smiled, as if her answer had pleased him. She glanced at Alex from the corner of her eye. He looked paler than ever and the snow clinging to his coat had turned pink, but if he was in pain, he didn't show it. He stood straight and tall, his gaze steady.

"Leave her alone, Jared," Alex said.

Jared ignored him and came closer, stopping an arm's length away.

"Abaddon is a demon. He's what other demons fear."

Lilly took a shallow breath, hoping he couldn't hear the dread rasping through it. "Glad I don't know him, then."

"Yes. You should be very glad. Hellhounds answer to Abaddon—or at least they used to."

Lilly knew her laugh would sound forced and denial would ring false, but he was watching her reactions and she couldn't pull off the stony countenance Alex had mastered.

"Interesting," she said with as much detachment as she could muster. "But I've never heard of Abaddon, and I don't believe in demons or hellhounds."

"I would've thought seeing was believing," Jared said.

"Maybe it is. If I see one or the other, I'll let you know."

His eyes narrowed. That was the only clue Lilly had that Jared meant to attack. Alex had seen it coming, though.

He moved swiftly, shoving her out of the way. She fell to the hard, cold ground just as a machete hissed through the air where her head would have been. She rolled as the stranger swung again, hacking down toward where she lay. Alex met the man head-on, weapon ready, blocking the blow. Lilly saw the flash of Alex's eyes a moment before he slammed into the stranger and both men crashed against the Range Rover.

"Get inside, Lilly," Alex shouted. "Go. Get out of here."

Lilly scrambled on her hands and knee around the front end of the SUV and staggered to her feet. Inside the cargo area, the dogs still barked like maniacs and scratched at the windows, racing from one to another and testing the strength of the mesh barrier that kept them confined. Her heart pounded like a damn war drum as she fumbled her keys from her pocket, slipping and skidding on the icy surface.

She chanced a look back at Alex, fighting for his life against his bigger, uninjured opponent.

Fighting for his life and *hers*.

Against one of his own.

The magnitude of it hit Lilly in waves as she wrenched open the driver's door, tossed the rifle in first, and flung herself in after it. She shut the door and locked it before she popped the glove box open and snatched her extra shells. Her fingers shook as she reloaded her gun.

The snow was coming down in droves now, so thick and blustery that she couldn't see through it. Alex and

41

Jared were blurry shapes in the pelting blizzard. What now? Drive off? *Leave* the man who'd helped her?

The dogs had steamed the windows. The sound of them in the enclosed space made her want to clap her hands over her ears, but bodies banged into the vehicle, rocking it, and she knew she had to act fast.

Lilly revved the engine, but she couldn't see behind her to reverse, couldn't go straight ahead unless she wanted to crash into the boulder. She could try a U-turn, but what if she hit them?

"Screw it," she said, and opened her door, coming around with the rifle locked and loaded. Jared had Alex pinned against the Range Rover, a short, lethal knife at his throat.

"Let him go," Lilly said in her best Clint Eastwood voice.

The stranger didn't even look up.

"Let him go or I start shooting. I may not look like much, but I killed three hellhounds I couldn't even see."

The words banked against the seething hostility and created a blockade that couldn't be ignored. She knew she'd just confessed to something this man considered a crime, but she also knew he'd already condemned her. She stared down the barrel and fired a warning shot that whizzed past his head and into the forest behind them.

The stranger hadn't expected it, but Alex had seen her in action and was ready. He slammed his forehead into Jared's nose, putting enough distance between them to bring his machete around. The blade sank deep into the stranger's chest. Jared looked down, stunned—by the pain or the reality, Lilly didn't know—and a wobbling step back landed him in a deep snowdrift. His knees gave and he sank.

Alex followed the other man, his expression hard as he leaned down to pull the machete out. He wiped the blade on Jared's sleeve and spat blood in the snow beside him.

"The rules don't apply to her," he said coldly.

His legs were unsteady when he faced Lilly again.

"Is he dead?" she whispered, looking on with wide eyes.

"As good as."

Alex hesitated and Lilly looked up in alarm. Was he going to stab the man in the heart and chop off his head now? Alex swayed again, blinking in the driving snow. Even if he wanted to, he obviously lacked the strength. Lilly rushed to the passenger side of the SUV and opened the door.

"Get in, Alex," she said, trying not to think of the man dying out in the cold. The man who'd meant to kill her. To kill both of them.

But Alex didn't move. Blood dripped from a new wound on his forehead, and his cheek was swollen, his eye puffy and bruised.

"I can't go with you, Lilly. More like him will be coming. For me."

And for her, if she stayed with Alex. She heard it in his voice, saw it in those startling eyes.

"I won't leave you to die," she said.

"If you don't leave me, *you* will die."

"So far I've managed to hold my own," she told him. "Don't make me shoot you, Alex. Get in."

He tried to smile, but it looked more like a grimace.

"Get in," she repeated, using the rifle to point for good measure.

Alex stared at her for a long moment without speaking. Confusion, respect, disbelief—all of it glimmered in his *On Golden Pond* eyes. He shook his head.

"Humans," he said with a hint of disgust.

But he got in.

CHAPTER FOUR

ALEX MIGHT BE hard to break, Lilly acknowledged, but he'd sustained some serious wounds, first from the hellhounds and then from his *friend*. By the time Lilly pulled up in front of her sister's cabin, his skin was ashen and his eyes dull. He was conscious enough to help as she got him out of the vehicle, but she had to manhandle him through the front door and onto the bench just inside. He faded in and out as she tugged off his boots and coat, trying to figure out what she should do next.

The cabin didn't have a wired phone and her cell kept searching but couldn't find a signal. Whistler Valley was a forty-five-minute drive from here in clear weather. She'd never make it in the storm. Even the short drive from where she'd parked to here had been harrowing.

Worried, she eyed Alex as the wind moaned. She didn't know how much of the blood covering him was his and how much belonged to the hellhounds or the man they'd left for dead in the freezing cold. Alex could have more serious injuries beneath the skin, too.

Frustrated, she surveyed her rustic surroundings. Amy hadn't tried to make the cabin into more than its name implied. It had a kitchen, a sitting room, a single bedroom, and a bathroom. She had furnished it herself and Lilly hadn't had the heart to change anything about it after she'd died.

At the front of the cabin was the sitting room, dominated by an overstuffed couch and chair with a battered coffee table between them. Amy's laptop, tablet, magazines, and books still cluttered the table, and a blanket was wadded up at the foot of the couch, Amy's slippers beneath it, just where she'd left them. Eventually Lilly would have to clear it all out, but she didn't have the heart for it yet. Now when it still felt like Amy might walk through the door at any minute with big smile and belly laugh.

The fireplace's massive stone surround stretched wall-to-wall with various built-in nooks of different sizes. Amy had used the space for books and snapshots of her dogs. Before her death, she'd added a framed picture of herself with her long-lost sister, Lilly. It held the place of honor on the mantel and it choked Lilly up every time she saw it. They'd had so little time together.

Lilly sighed and looked back at the wounded man, still seated on the bench, his head lolled back against the wall and his eyes closed. His chest rose and fell unevenly, but she didn't hear the rattling sound of death that had chased every breath Amy had taken before she'd died. Lilly needed to move Alex to the couch somehow, though, where he could lie down and she could attempt to patch him up.

"Alex," she said as she approached him. But his eyes remained closed. "Come on, Alex. Stand up. Let's get you to the couch and then you can rest."

His eyes opened, but they were unfocused. Knowing she might not get more than that out of him, she sat beside him, slung his arm over her shoulder, and stood, forcing him up with her. He weighed a ton and she'd never have succeeded if he hadn't roused enough to help. They danced an awkward tango across the floor, listing from side to side. The dogs helped, which meant they made every effort to trip them both. By the time they reached the couch, she could do little more than maneuver him in the right direction and push. He collapsed in a heap on the big, soft cushions.

"You still with me?" she asked as she swung his legs up.

She didn't expect an answer, but he muttered, "Not dead, if that's what you mean."

Pretty much exactly what she'd meant. She hurried back to the front door and locked it, checking the dead bolt twice. Alex gave a dry laugh.

"That won't stop anything."

"Shut up," she said.

In seconds, she had a fire going and some water boiling. She hung her coat on the hook next to Alex's and shoved her boots under the bench beside his. It made her pause, the sight of the two pairs. Like they belonged together. She tried to ignore the longing that sparked out of nowhere. She didn't know this man, and he certainly wasn't the mate to her North Face boots. According to him, he wasn't even human. With a scowl, she pulled Amy's impressive first aid kit out of the closet and set it on the coffee table.

Blood had soaked his flannel shirt and Lilly carefully stripped him of it. He helped with silent and grim determination, never looking away from her face as she revealed a broad, muscled chest, strong arms, and flat abdomen. Necessary or not, she felt awkward with her fingers at his fly, more so when he lifted his hips so she could pull off his pants and gain access to the wound on his thigh. It was impossible not to notice the ripple of muscle, the strip of flesh between his belly button and the elastic of his briefs. A dark arrow of silky hair drew her eyes downward.

He might not be human . . . He might not even consider himself a man . . . But he sure as hell looked like one to Lilly.

She glanced at his face. His eyes were shut now, his breathing deep.

She surveyed his body, trying to be as clinical as possible. A large, angry bite stood out on his ribs. She gently cleaned the wound with hot water and a soft cloth before putting disinfectant and a bandage over it. Blood had splattered his abdomen, and with perhaps a little more attention to detail than needed, she cleaned that, too, smoothing the supple skin with her fingertips.

She glanced up again and found him watching her. Her hand rested against his belly, where it had no business being. Blushing so hard it hurt, she snatched it away.

"You said you weren't a man," she exclaimed, and then wanted to cover her head with a blanket and die.

"Never said I wasn't male," he answered darkly and closed his eyes again. "Give me a couple of hours and I'll prove it."

Lilly stared at him, her mouth open and a whole host of conflict in her chest. She cleared her throat. "That won't be necessary," she said primly.

He gave a soft, rumbling laugh and then groaned.

After that, Lilly kept her hands busy in more appropriate ways.

She worked methodically, first cleaning all his wounds. She was no doctor, but she'd learned fundamental first aid around the same time she'd learned to shoot—after her adoptive parents had been murdered in their home when she was seventeen. But she didn't want to think about that now.

She scanned Alex's body once more after cleaning him up. His arm bore the worst of the wounds and was probably the main source of the blood. Bites and bruises covered it, and she worried that he needed stitches, but that was more than she could do. She used butterfly bandages instead and wrapped it twice with gauze. Once cleaned, the wound on his thigh wasn't as bad as she'd expected, and she bandaged it without too much effort.

She was exhausted by the time she finished. Standing, she stretched the tight muscles in her neck and back before walking to the window. Snow dropped from the sky in a thick blanket that showed no signs of easing. Even if it stopped during the night, they would likely be stranded for days.

At least their tracks would be covered. Anyone who tried to find them would be left without a trail to follow

Relieved that they were safe for now, she left Alex to rest while she took a shower, washing away the stench of fear and the splatter of blood. Clean and too tired to do anything else, Lilly added wood to the fire, curled up in the chair next to the couch where Alex lay, and closed her eyes. She was asleep in minutes.

CHAPTER FIVE

ALEX SAW LILLY the moment he opened his eyes. She slept on an overstuffed chair beside him, her head on the armrest closest to where he lay, her legs dangling over the other side. She managed to look comfortable, though he couldn't figure out how it was possible. Like a kitten, curled into an impossibly small space.

The fire she must've started had burned low, but embers still glowed in the ash. The room was chilly, but the blanket she'd put over him was warm. Its twin covered Lilly. On the floor beside her, four dogs watched him from their beds. A fluffy head popped up from the gap behind Lilly's bent knees. Harley, she'd called that one.

He watched her silently. Her hair looked like burnished gold in the muted light, so silky he yearned to reach out and touch it. Her chinks were pink, her lashes lace against them. He wanted to bury his face in the crook between her shoulder and neck, and breathe in the scent he'd only managed to catch in passing so far. He hadn't come to dally with humans, but with this one . . . Forbidden or not, he definitely wanted to dally.

He closed his eyes, remembering the soft brush of her fingers against his skin. Her face had been flushed as she touched him then, too, her eyes jewel-bright. Her thoughts had laced the air between them, rousing him from semi consciousness with a bite of longing that he'd felt deep inside.

He should be glad he hadn't had the strength to answer it with his own desire.

He winced as he sat up. During the night, blood had soaked through his bandages, but now it appeared that the bleeding had stopped and the gauze had dried. Even where his arm had been sliced. That one hurt the most, but it was the kind of pain that came with healing, not infection. He'd survived enough injuries to know the difference. He flexed his fingers and wondered where Lilly had learned to dress a wound so efficiently.

He took a steady breath and looked around the small cabin. The room had a strange cast to it, a sickly green-gray that pulled him from the couch to make his slow and painful way to the window. The world outside was a blustering white mess beneath a sky so gray and frigid it blocked out the sun and distorted its glow. The storm hadn't eased at all. If anything, night had given it power that even dawn couldn't diminish.

The biggest dog—Belle—came to him with a soft whine. The others followed, even the ridiculous small one. As if hearing the thought, Harley showed Alex his teeth.

"Going to take more than that," Alex murmured, amused.

"They want out," a sleepy voice said.

He glanced at Lilly, who was still curled in her chair, and then down at himself, wearing nothing but his briefs.

"Do they need an escort?"

She sat up and looked at him, her crystalline gaze taking in every inch of his naked skin from bare feet up the length of him to his chin. She lingered on his mouth before her smoldering gaze met his. Her face turned red, and Alex crossed his hands in front of his hips to hide the response he couldn't control.

"Have you heard anything out there?" she asked.

Like the hellhounds she couldn't hear or see?

He shook his head. "This storm is bad. I don't think even hellhounds can track in this."

She looked relieved. He'd always heard that hellhounds were made for the fires of hell, not the bitter cold of winter, but he doubted she'd feel reassured by the information. They'd held their own yesterday and it had been damn cold then. It made him wonder what other false information he'd been given.

Lilly stretched, an uninhibited movement that made Alex's muscles tighten. Her back arched and her toes pointed. She looked so sleepy and soft that he could almost imagine what it would feel like to hold her, to know her taste.

She was staring at him again, her mouth slightly open now. Her beautiful eyes, wide.

Could all the beings in this house read his thoughts?

The desire to act on his urges nearly pulled him across the room, but the toy dog at his feet yipped, reminding Alex that he was waiting to go out. Lilly stood and crossed the room to the door. She wore clingy pants that accented her shape and a big T-shirt with a wide neck that gaped at her shoulder and hugged her breasts.

"Porch," she said in a stern voice. The five dogs sat very still and watched her obediently, all but nodding *okay* before she let them out.

Alex came to stand behind her as the dogs raced down the stairs to take care of their business within a foot of the porch. She waited for them in front of the open door, her body warm despite the cold blast that blustered its way inside. He felt her stiffen at his nearness, then yield in the same compelling moment. She wanted to lean back; she thought she should move away. Before she could overthink it, Alex stepped closer until he was touching her, chest to shoulder blades, hips a whisper from her round behind. It was a blissful torture that he wished would never end.

But in seconds the dogs were back in the house. Each one of them paused to shake a shower of snow at him as they passed by.

Lilly swung the door shut, but she didn't move away. Neither did he.

"They obeyed," she said, her voice filled with breath and nervousness. "Usually they don't. Not like they did when Amy talked to them."

"Oh." Because she seemed to be waiting for a response.

It was hard to think with her so close. Her hair smelled of apples and looked too silky not to touch. He moved his fingers through it gently, letting the tips scrape her scalp before he pushed it aside, baring the curve of her shoulder where the round neck of her shirt was loose. He felt her catch her breath.

"The storm hasn't let up at all," she said.

In case he hadn't noticed, hadn't considered that he might be stranded here for days. With her.

He lowered his head and she tilted hers to the side, giving him access to the graceful slope of her neck. He let his breath caress the satiny skin, afraid if he did more, he wouldn't be able to stop. He should back away, but he couldn't seem to do it.

"Maybe they won't be able to find us," she said. "Whoever comes looking for you."

The words held a wistfulness that wrapped around his senses. Maybe they wouldn't be found . . . It was an idea so intoxicating and forbidden that it made him close his eyes and ground himself in reality.

"They'll find me," he said grimly. "But I'll be long gone from here when they do."

She spun to face him. The top of her head came to his chin, and he wanted to tuck her into the curve of his body and shield her from anything that meant her harm. But that wouldn't work when it was Alex's presence that placed her in harm's way. She stared at him, confusion sharing space with something that might be anger.

At him? At the situation? At herself?

"You're not here to protect us, are you, Alex?" she asked, her voice husky. "Humans, I mean."

"Did you really think I was?"

She didn't answer. He wished she would. For reasons he didn't understand, he wished the truth could match her expectations.

"So why do you want to kill the hellhounds? Why do you care if they eat up the natives?"

"It's not natural."

"Because human's aren't meant to know they exist," she finished for him, her voice flat. "Not because you give a damn if they kill us."

The disappointment in her voice hung in the quiet. He hated that he cared.

"What are they doing up here in the middle of nowhere anyway?" she went on. "You said they were left behind. This seems an unlikely place to be in the first place."

"We think they made their way up north from the outskirts of the city."

"Hiding?"

"They're smart creatures."

A shiver went through her. "Have you been tracking them for long?"

"No. Yesterday, there was a sighting not far from here and they sent us to handle it. But we had no idea what we'd be facing. We expected a handful of hounds, not a whole pack," he said. "All we knew was that we needed to get close enough for them to smell us and they'd come."

Her eyes rounded and her jaw dropped. "You're not serious."

"I am."

"Well, that's a great plan if you want to get *eaten*."

The exclamation caught him by surprise. Before he could respond, she went on.

"If you want to hunt *them*, however, you have to see them before they know you're there."

"And how many hellhounds have you hunted?" he asked derisively.

"It doesn't matter what you're hunting. If they see you first, they have the advantage."

"And you're an expert because?"

"I watch the Discovery Channel and I have five dogs, in case you hadn't noticed."

"Hellhounds are not dogs, not that you know a damn thing about them, either."

She scowled. He was right and they both knew it.

"But what *are* hellhounds exactly?"

"If I said *demons* would you sleep better knowing?"

She recoiled. He knew she couldn't help it.

"Why do you ask me questions when you know you'll hate the answers?" he asked.

"I hate not knowing more," she said with raised brows.

A smile tugged the corner of his mouth. "Do you practice that look in the mirror?"

"What look?"

"The one that hides your fear."

"What makes you think I'm afraid?"

"You're too intelligent not to be."

She didn't want to be pleased by the backhanded compliment he hadn't meant to give. But she was. He could see it in her startled eyes, in the way she tried to conceal it by looking away.

She sniffed. "I'm not hiding anything. I have a gun and I know how to use it."

"So brave."

"Says the man whose ass I saved."

He laughed, and for a moment, she seemed fascinated by the sight and sound of it. Her stare made his muscles tighten all over again. He wanted to touch her. He wanted more than that.

"So that's it?" she asked in a voice that wasn't quite steady. "You zip in, round up demons, kill them, and fly away home, wherever that is? What does that make you? An exterminator?"

His smile faded in the face of his true circumstances. "Well, right now I'm an outlaw."

Based on her expression, he guessed that she hadn't yet considered the impact of what he'd done, fighting one of his own to protect her. *Killing* Jared. He could scarcely believe it himself, but Alex had been enraged when Jared had attacked Lilly. His brain had disconnected and all he'd been able to think was how she'd come to his aid without thought for her own safety. The need to protect her had been strong and instinctive.

"An outlaw," she said in a small voice. "Because of me."

He shook his head. "Jared . . . he was always angry. Always blaming everyone else for his problems. It made him dangerous. To everyone."

"You told me you were dangerous, too."

Alex didn't know how to respond to that. It was true when he'd said it. It was still true now.

"Who *are* you, Alex?"

The question was soft, lilting. He knew she didn't expect an answer from him. But she hoped. He heard it in the way she'd rushed the words, her voice so uncertain.

He'd told her he wasn't human. He'd told her he wasn't a man. She should be hiding under the bed instead of teasing him with her feather light touches and elusive scent. She glanced up and he found himself falling into the shimmer of her eyes. Eyes that spoke to him, to some different version of him. One he wanted to be.

His throat felt tight when he spoke. "I'm a soldier, Lilly, and I just killed someone on my own side. Others will come looking for me."

"I'm sorry."

"It's not your fault. Caleb was a friend, but Jared never was. He had too many issues, especially with humans. He never missed an opportunity to punish them. I couldn't let him hurt you, though. Not after you'd saved my life."

"Do you have issues with humans, Alex?"

He hadn't seen the question coming, and he had no idea how to answer it. Did he? It wasn't a simple yes or no. Humans had freedoms that he'd never known, choices he'd never had the chance to make. But did he harbor resentment because of it?

He cleared his throat. "No issues," he said.

Lilly's eyes called him a liar, but she didn't say the word aloud, nor did she voice any of the questions he saw lurking in those blue depths.

"I just need to be sure I'm gone before they come looking for me. I don't want you involved any more than you already are."

"What will you do next?"

"I don't know."

She placed her hand on his chest, palm soft against his bare skin. Could she feel how hard his heart was beating?

"Why did you do that?" she asked. "Why did you take such a risk to help me, I mean?"

"I don't know that, either."

It was an answer that didn't satisfy either one of them. She must have heard the reluctance in his tone, the resistance. The denial when she deserved the truth. She began to pull away and he stopped her, covering her hand with his.

"I wanted . . . I knew . . . I had to protect you. I didn't even think about it. I couldn't stand the thought those blue eyes . . . hurt." Of life fading from them, of the sparkle going out.

The confession was rife with honesty that, for once, he didn't try to hide. She stared at him, lips parted in muted shock.

"I wanted to keep you safe."

The lavender in her eyes became gray and somber, and he feared she was going to cry.

"What's wrong?" he asked. Because clearly something was. "Why did that make you sad?"

She looked away, but Alex turned her face back to his. Her fake smile made him shake his head.

"I'm not sad," she said in a choked voice. "It's just . . . It's . . . I haven't had many protectors in my life." She glanced away again. "Thank you."

The words sank deep inside him, a pearl falling to the soft sediments of his soul. He hadn't had many protectors, either. He was glad he'd been one for her.

"You realize that I'm the reason you needed protection, right?" he teased.

"Don't do that," she said. "Don't belittle it."

Her shoulder lifted in a small, meaningless gesture. Except, right then, it was filled with meaning. About what he'd done, about what it meant to her, about the current that raced through him whenever she touched him.

He wanted to look into her face. He needed the cues of expression, of her shadowed eyes to understand this deeply layered conversation. But she'd be the one to see too much. She'd know what it meant, the yearning inside him. The desire to pull her against him and make her his.

Even the idea was crazy. He was not meant for this world or this woman. Creatures of the Beyond didn't mate like humans. They fornicated—of course they did—but that wasn't what he wanted to do with Lilly and he knew it.

The thought led him down a dangerous path.

She sighed and stepped away from him. He forced himself to let her go, but he didn't want to. Silently, she moved to the table and reached for the white box with a red cross on its lid sitting on top of it.

"How do you feel?" she asked, not looking at him.

He should be grateful that she'd changed the subject, that she'd moved them both to safer ground.

But he wasn't.

"I feel like I've been chewed up by a pack of hellhounds."

She almost smiled as she reached for a small bottle and shook two capsules out. "Take these and sit down so I can check your bandages."

"What are they?"

"Roofies."

"What?"

"Just kidding. Amoxicillin. An antibiotic for infection. You might need a rabies shot, too. It'd probably be a good idea to get one once the snow clears enough to get to a doctor. Sit."

He took the pills and did as she'd said. He tried not to feel the soft brush of her fingers against his skin while she examined him, but he'd have had better luck trying not to breathe.

"I think the bleeding has stopped," she said, golden head bent. "That's good."

He was glad she thought so, but it hurt like a son of a bitch.

She worked quietly, pulling off the old bandages, then cleaning the wounds with something that stung before covering them again with clean gauze. When she finished, she met his eyes. He didn't know how to reconcile or subdue all the feelings inside him.

He took her hand in his. Her fingers were soft, small in his grasp. It felt overwhelmingly intimate to be touching her like this, but Alex didn't understand why. Hands shouldn't be so sensitive, so . . . personal.

"You can't talk about what you saw yesterday, Lilly. Not to anyone. Not ever."

"I understand."

She held his gaze for a moment, her fingers moving against his. A lump had formed in his chest, and Alex reluctantly released her hand and looked away.

After a moment, Lilly asked, "Will you confess or will they already know how your people died? When they find you, I mean."

The question was a good one, but he hadn't decided how to handle it when the time came. Protectors were told that they'd be under constant surveillance when they were on Earth. Alex had always believed it to be true, but now he had his doubts.

When he didn't answer, Lilly asked another question. She had them stockpiled, it seemed. "So this army you're in . . . did you sign up or were you drafted?"

"Neither. We're bred to protect the Beyond," he said simply.

Disapproval pulled her brows and narrowed her eyes. "Bred? That's barbaric."

"I live in a world of demons, Lilly."

She shuddered. "I can't wrap my head around this place you're from."

"Yet another reason why you're not supposed to know it exists. Outsiders can never understand it. But trying to keep it secret is like trying to make air hold still. Humans see things, hear things . . . They talk." He shook his head. "Believe it or not, the Beyond and Earth have the same creator but the differences between here and there are many."

"You don't seem that different."

"I'm an exception. I look like you, talk like you, and act like you so I can infiltrate your world undetected."

"What about when you go home?"

He couldn't hold her gaze. Lilly was far too perceptive not to see through his canned explanation to the feelings even he didn't quite understand.

"Soldiers, like me, live in a replica of your world. We are immersed in your culture, your ways."

"And you never get to leave it and go home? You know, see the family?"

"We have no family."

"What about when you were little?"

His smile felt brittle. "My earliest memories are of conditioning. Watching human pop culture. Practicing it. Pretending. We had drill sergeants instead of parents."

Her full lips drew into a flat line. She didn't like that answer, either, he guessed.

"We are promised afterlife if we die in glory," he tacked on, as if that would make the truth of it any better.

"And if you don't die in glory?"

He shrugged again. He wasn't entirely sure—only knew that it wouldn't be pleasant. "The unknown is a good motivator. Don't you live the same way? Hoping that when your judgment day comes you won't be found lacking?"

"I suppose." She frowned, working through another question, no doubt. "How are you supposed to get back anyhow? Is there a secret passageway?"

Her sarcasm made him scowl. "I can't answer that."

"I'm right, aren't I?"

"It's not for humans to know."

He hadn't meant to sound so hostile, but his frustration made his voice loud and his tone sharp. Before he could figure out how to temper the harshness, she looked away, hiding her hurt, shutting him out. He was beginning to learn that was her way.

"Is it okay to ask about your people or leaders or whatever you call them . . . or are they top secret, as well? Too important for a lowly human like me? Are they omnipotent, like God?"

"This whole conversation is not 'okay.' It's dangerous for you to know these things, Lilly."

"So they are omnipotent. They're watching us now."

"No," he said with a resigned sigh. "At least I don't think so."

"Then for all they know, you're down here fighting the good fight. Jared and Caleb will still get afterlives, right? They died in their own kind of glory, fighting for what they believed in."

She was right, of course, but Alex was hazy on the logistics of how the afterlife worked. He had a comical vision of a bearded being with a checklist waiting at the gates. No matter how it was written, though, his fellow Protectors had died in duty.

For now, that's all anyone could know. It made him feel better.

He looked at Lilly. "So what are you, an expert on afterlife?"

"Sorta. I'm a marketing advisor for a small health food chain."

He stared at her for a moment before he realized she'd meant the *sorta* as a joke. But he was too surprised to laugh. A marketing advisor? Lilly? It seemed so ordinary, and Lilly . . . Lilly was the opposite of ordinary.

"Health food?" he disparaged. "Does that mean you don't eat meat?"

She shook her head guiltily, adding, "Not veal, though." Like it that made up for her transgression.

She smoothed the edges of the last bandage and stood. Alex stood, too. He should move away. And now. Because having her within touching distance seemed to be destroying all his common sense.

"The longer I stay, the worse it will be," he said, trying to infuse the words with the power to make him leave.

"Who are you trying to convince, Alex? You or me?"

"You've got a smart mouth," he said. "You know that?"

"I might have heard it a time or two."

She stared at him with those lavender-blue eyes and all he could think about was tasting that smart mouth. One kiss, that would be enough, he told himself.

But she met him halfway as he leaned toward her and he knew it was a lie.

CHAPTER SIX

ALEX KISSED HER slowly. He'd meant to be quick. A small sample and then walk away. But lips and breath and tongue combined to shut down his brain. She was like a drug that spread rapidly through his system. Suddenly, *not* touching her everywhere seemed like the worst choice he could make.

He pulled back and stared into her eyes. She looked startled but aroused, wary but very willing. She listed forward, her face turned up, her hands warm on his bare chest, and Alex couldn't have denied what he wanted any more than he could turn back time.

In an instant, the decision was made.

It had been since he'd first held her in the woods. Maybe everything he'd done since that moment had been a way to get here. With her.

His forehead touched hers, and their noses aligned as he stilled, letting her breath become his, giving it back with his own. So intimate, the sharing. Exotic, unexpected, addicting. Thunder and lightning struck at ancestral instincts he hadn't known he possessed. She pressed against him, his briefs a thin barrier for the hardness straining to be released. Every part of him responded to her actions, to her reactions, and the way they spurred his own.

What did it mean that he'd brought his hands to her face and found skin so soft he had to brush his lips over it? Press his nose into its sweetness? He thought he could stand there and kiss her for hours and never grow tired of the way she felt, the way she tasted?

She seemed to be seeking something. A touch? A word? He wanted to give it to her, whatever it was, and the thought pulled him back. Her eyes glittered bright blue and diamond-like from between her thick lashes. Her hair was messed up, her cheeks chilled, but she felt like a flame in his hands. Fluid. Dangerous.

Make her choose you . . .

The thought felt ancient, a rumbling drum down a sacred mountain. It urged him to coax, to crowd, to *claim.*

He tried to tell himself he didn't want that, but his body had ceased to listen to his brain.

He kissed her while her breath was shallow. Her breasts lifted in welcome, her hands in his hair, touching his neck. His chest tightened, locking up with sensation. He'd forgotten how to breathe at all.

Where was his survival instinct? Lost in the sexual haze she cast over him?

Nothing made sense but the way she felt against his skin. With her arms tight around his neck, she arched closer.

If he'd had any doubt, he understood now: this would be nothing like fornication.

He backed her into the bedroom, his lips on hers, holding her so close that his bare thigh brushed between hers with each step. Their legs bumped into the mattress and Lilly pulled him down on top of her.

The feeling of settling into her softness, into an embrace that felt so right, made him groan. The sound came from deep in his throat, primal vulnerable…both at once. Lilly met his eyes, and for a moment, indecision gleamed in hers. He shook his head, needing to banish it.

She wanted him and he wanted her. There was no room for indecision.

It seemed she heard him, and against all reason, she agreed. She raised her arms so he could pull off her shirt, then wrapped them back around his shoulders while he kissed his way to the white bra that held her breasts. He unfastened it and cupped them in his hands while he caught her mouth in another a kiss, intent on stealing any will to resist. He had only a short time here. A few days, a week if he was very lucky. He'd dreaded this journey. Now he didn't want it to end.

"Alex," she breathed against his mouth.

"Don't say no," he breathed back. "Please, don't say no."

She laughed. "I don't think I know that word anymore."

Relief made him dizzy; desire made him rush when he wanted to linger. He tugged off her pants, hooking her flowered panties with his thumbs and drawing them over her silky legs. In seconds, he was stripped, as well.

For a moment, he could only stare at her. She was naked and perfect in every way imaginable. The winter light turned her skin to pearl and caressed the enticing curves and dips of her body. Her blond hair spilled over the pillow. She was satiny-soft in places that seduced him. She shocked his senses and addled his brain until the only thing Alex knew for certain was that whatever he did next, he needed to make sure she'd want him to do it again.

He kissed her deeply, pulling her closer as he moved over her. He was shaking as their gazes locked. Slowly, reverently, he thrust into her heat, into her body. She didn't look away. Neither did he, not even when it felt like she might be able to see into his soul.

Tomorrow he'd be gone, but right now he was here, on fire. Consumed by her.

He felt powerful, braced above her, skin to skin, chests moving fast, hearts moving faster. He felt defenseless, turned inside out. He wanted to slow down but her hands urged him on, her knees rising to frame his hips, her mouth restless beneath his.

Nothing else mattered. There was only Lilly, with her moonlit skin and sunrise eyes. Lilly, with her melting kisses and arched body. His focus centered on the thrust of his hips, the bow of her spine, the way her feet locked at the small of his back and her head tossed as he rocked against her, inside her. *Pleasure* was too basic a word for what he felt. *Pain* came closer but omitted the bliss that grew and grew until it defined him.

Lilly's orgasm came with a husky cry and a rush of damp heat that pushed him over the edge after her. A moment later, Alex came so hard he couldn't breathe as the pleasure and pain merged inside him. He'd never felt anything so intense. He held her, both of them panting, until they could breathe again. He tried to loosen his hold then, afraid he'd crushed her beneath him, but she pulled him back, her legs entwined with his as she continued to pulse around him.

Finally, his heart slowed and he rolled beside her on the bed, tucking her into the curve of his body. They lay there quietly for a while. Replete. But thoughts and recriminations had already begun to crowd in. What was he thinking? This was a human female in his arms! Something so far out of his reach—so *forbidden*—that even now, he couldn't imagine that he'd dared to touch her in the first place.

Her thoughts must have run parallel to his own for he sensed her withdrawal before he felt her move away. He told himself he was relieved.

CHAPTER SEVEN

LILLY DRESSED HASTILY, aware of his hot gaze on her as she bent to pull on fresh underwear and a pair of yoga pants. Embarrassed, she fumbled with her bra and a clean shirt. She shrugged a sweatshirt over it all and gathered the pieces of her discarded clothing to toss into the laundry basket.

Anything to avoid looking at the naked man in her bed. Because when she looked at him, she wanted to climb back in.

And no good could come of that.

She didn't regret what she'd done. Which wasn't the same as saying it had been a good choice. Like taking a bite of a donut when the whole box was waiting to be devoured. Now she'd had a taste and, of course, she wanted more. A voice in her head was already trying to convince her that the damage was done, so why not enjoy it? There'd be plenty of time for regrets later.

She gave him one last look and caught him watching her in that searching way of his. There was a grim set to his jaw and a guarded gleam in his eyes. What was he thinking?

Maybe this was what he did. Earth girls were easy, right?

No, she didn't believe this had been casual for him, either. That had been crazy, brain-disconnected-hormones-in-charge sex. Her heart still hadn't returned to its normal pace. But wanting more was only going to make it harder when he left. And he would.

He'd been promised afterlife in return for the privilege of getting himself killed by hellhounds. How could she compete with that? Had she not been on that trail yesterday, they wouldn't have even met.

She took a deep breath. "I need some coffee. You?"

He rubbed his face and nodded, eyeing her like he was trying to figure out what she might be thinking, too. She let him wonder. Her thoughts were too scattered, stretching the gamut of her emotions, most of them even *she* didn't understand. If he had any inkling of what was going on in her head, he'd be heading for the hills. Literally.

"Not that I'm complaining," she said over her shoulder as she headed out of the bedroom, "but if you want some pants, I'm pretty sure my sister had a live-in boyfriend for a while. He left some clothes."

"Lilly," he said.

"I don't know what size they are," she rushed on before he could say whatever was coming next, "but they're better than the ones I stripped off you last night. At least until they get washed. Check in the chest, bottom drawer. Can't miss them."

She didn't stop moving until she reached the kitchen. She was breathless, close to tears, bordering anger, and still turned on. Her own confusion over the devastating emotional tornado inside made her feel so vulnerable that she needed distance from him.

None of what she felt was his fault, yet somehow, *all of it* was his fault.

"Welcome to the human female," she muttered beneath her breath.

A few seconds later, she heard Alex let loose a frustrated sigh and pad to the chest of drawers. She tried not to listen as he opened and shut it or when he went into the small bathroom and started the shower, but she couldn't mute her awareness of him.

"You are so screwed," she muttered.

Because she wanted him, this stranger who claimed he wasn't human, who told crazy stories of some Beyond and deathly creatures that left bloody gashes all over his body even though she couldn't see them. Despite it all, she wanted him like she'd never wanted any man before. She'd just had him and she wanted more. When he'd stood behind her earlier, his chest a breath away from her back, when he'd smoothed her hair and touched her shoulder, she'd practically melted to the floor. And he hadn't even kissed her yet.

I never said I wasn't male.

Understatement of the century. He was so male that he'd fine-tuned every feminine response inside her, and left her waiting for him to do it again.

He found her in the kitchen just as the coffee finished brewing. Lilly pretended that his presence didn't interrupt the time-space continuum between her brain and her sex, but she'd never been a great pretender. Besides, he could probably feel the heat coming off her in waves.

In hopes of hiding it, she busied herself filling cups, adding cream to hers. She inhaled the brew, trying not to notice how good he smelled—soap, shampoo, and Alex. She wanted to press her nose to his chest and just breathe. She flicked a glance in his direction. He wore a pair of jeans belted at the waist and a flannel shirt that hung loosely over his broad shoulders. She knew what kind of muscles she'd feel under that fabric if she touched him.

And she wanted to touch him.

Socks covered his feet and a bland expression hid his thoughts from her. But in her mind, he was still stripped and taut with desire, those eyes so hot they'd deep-fried her common sense.

"Your sister's friend had about sixty pounds on me," he said with a tight smile.

Lilly was willing to wager that's all he had on Alex. Even dark and broody, he was the sexiest man—or male, she guessed—she'd ever met. He made her feel giddy whenever he was near her. She'd seen other women react that way to men, but she'd never felt anything like the yearning that roared to life just being in the same room with him.

She took a deep breath and tried to focus. "Are you hungry?"

"Is that what we do next? Eat?"

His gaze snared hers again, and she was sucked in by the beauty of his eyes. What color *were* they? Brown was too mild, green too precise, and hazel not nearly vivid enough. The short fringe of black lash set them off and made them all the more mesmerizing.

She forced herself back to reality and cleared her throat. "It is if you're hungry."

He came around the counter and took the coffee cup Lilly had filled for him while she made a production of gathering the eggs, a skillet, and utensils. She couldn't help it. She felt all twisted up inside.

She rolled her eyes at herself. What was *wrong* with her? She didn't even know this man. But perhaps that was the root of the problem. She *wanted* to know him, but even though he'd shared some of his secrets, she knew there was so much more he kept hidden inside. . Did he expect her to run to the authorities and tell them she knew where the portal to this Beyond was if he dared to share it with her? Did he think she was nuts?

"There's a rendezvous point," he said to her back. "That's where I'm to go when my mission is complete."

His voice was so deep, it sent chills down her spine. And his words were so close to her thoughts that she turned, wondering if she'd been talking out loud without realizing it.

He leaned against the counter, long legs stretched in front of him, mug held between his big hands. His hair was still wet, his jaw shadowed. He looked dangerous and sexy, and she suspected that if he said, *Again?* she'd jump his bones right there on the kitchen floor.

She was such a fool. An awkward horsey laugh escaped her, followed by a scalding blush. Hopefully, he wouldn't pluck *that* thought out of her head . . . or maybe, hopefully, he would.

She cleared her throat. "The super secret passageway?" she said.

As usual, it felt like he was seeing right through her to her gooey, confused, libido-driven center. Maybe that was his superpower. That and really great sex.

She turned back to her eggs, scrambling them with more aggression than they deserved. "So how far away is it?"

"A couple of miles. There's a small valley west of here. Secluded, hard to see from above."

He spoke carefully, as if he knew all the turmoil she was trying so hard to disguise. Having whipped the eggs into submission, she poured them into the now-hot skillet.

"Will it take you long to get home? To the Beyond?"

"Seconds," he answered.

"Well that's disturbing. I thought it would be more. That makes it seem like we're neighbors." Another thought occurred to her. "Do you come here all the time?"

"No," he answered, shaking his head. "And chances are I won't be back. Generally, I'm kept busy in the Beyond."

"You have people to protect there, too? I guess they wouldn't be people. Citizens . . . whatever you call them. Angels, maybe?"

He stared at her, his expression pained.

"Oh. That again. You'd have to kill me if you told me."

"Stop it, Lilly."

Something in his tone defused her anger. Maybe it was the resignation. Maybe it was the caution. Maybe it had nothing to do with Alex and everything to do with Lilly. She recognized her own defense mechanisms kicking in. She'd let him see inside her, and now she resented him for it.

She let out a sigh and nodded.

Alex looked away as he spoke. "I told you, rumors of the Beyond have leaked into the human world. Humans have a way of finding out things they'd be better off not knowing."

He gave her a speaking glance that she chose to ignore.

"Human nature makes you try to explain what you don't understand. That's where your ideas of gods and demons, heaven and hell all come into play. In some ways you're right. It's all that. Heaven, hell . . . all the outliers that meet in the middle."

Outliers. "Like hellhounds."

She chanced a look over her shoulder. Beneath all that sexy, Alex looked tired and sore, battered to the bone. He leaned his head back and turned his face to the ceiling.

"Like hellhounds," he agreed wearily.

"So are you one of the outliers, too?" she asked.

He shook his head, thought about it, and shrugged. Great. He didn't even know.

"The middle—the in-between—where it all meets? It's not a nice place. I make sure everyone stays on their own side of the fence."

"And when they get out, you round them up and kill them."

"It's what I do."

"When they aren't on top of you, you mean."

He grinned. A devastating grin that she felt right down to her toes.

"This may be hard to believe," he said, "but it doesn't usually play that way. Not with me."

No. It wasn't hard to believe at all. She'd had an unimpeded view of all his muscle and strength. It was a wonder the stupid hellhounds hadn't bolted as soon as they saw him.

"Why did you run away?" he asked in a husky voice.

She didn't need him to explain what he was referring to. She'd left the bed like it was on fire. What he didn't realize was that she'd been the one burning.

"Is it because of what I am?" he asked, his voice low and troubled. "What I'm not . . ."

Human. That's what he meant.

"Well, that and the fact that you're a stranger. You may find this hard to believe, but what just happened between us . . . it doesn't usually play that way. Not with me."

His eyes glittered with amusement, but his question came with a serious tone. "Why did you do it, then?"

A play on her words this time. She'd asked the same thing when Alex said he'd made himself an outlaw by protecting her from Jared.

They stared at one another, the query hanging heavy between them. How could she answer? She didn't understand this attraction herself. The physical aspect was obvious, of course; she would have noticed Alex under any circumstance. But there was something deeper than beautiful eyes and a muscled body that drew her to him.

Maybe it was the way he listened when she talked. Maybe it was the way he seemed to hear more than just the words she spoke. Her entire life she'd felt . . . lost. Abandoned children usually did. And even though she'd been taken in by good, loving people, she'd lost them, too.

Lilly had moved on, forged a life. She had friends, if not family, but she'd never had the permanence of blood relations, something that connected her by its very existence. Until her sister had appeared without warning. For a short, poignant time, Lilly had been part of something more. Then Amy had died and Lilly had felt so empty and alone. The kind of empty that never went away.

But now here was Alex, and Lilly felt a little less hollow. She felt hopeful. He understood what it meant to stand against the tide while it sucked everything you valued out to sea. She felt bonded with him, paired somehow. And it scared the hell out of her.

"Why don't you have a mate?" he asked.

The question froze her and pricked at her already jumbled emotions. It was cruel and honest and too painful to answer. She looked away, hurt. Angry that she was hurt.

"Not every woman wants a mate," she said with a cool toss of her head.

He wasn't fooled. She could feel that searching stare tracking her movements, seeing beneath the surface.

Two pieces of browned bread popped up from the toaster. Glad for the distraction, Lilly buttered them, scooped up some scrambled eggs and arranged them both on plates. She handed one to Alex, taking the other for herself. He gave her a quizzical glance but didn't repeat his question. Somehow, she managed to hide her relief.

They sat at the small table in the kitchen and ate in silence, avoiding each other's eyes. There'd been no dinner the night before and they were both hungry. Lilly caught herself wolfing her eggs and made an effort to slow down, but Alex shoveled it in at the same pace, unaware of her inner etiquette lecture, so she just let herself eat.

Her tension drained as she filled her stomach, and by the time they'd both finished, she was ready to move away from the emotional volcano, but she still had questions she wanted answered.

"Why can't humans know about the Beyond, Alex?" she asked as he pushed away from the table. "Why is it so important to keep us in the dark?"

He shook his head, eyes at half-mast. But she felt the resistance running through him. It ignited a fuse inside Lilly that was already too short. He'd either deflect or evade. He didn't trust her. He didn't know her. She didn't know him, either, regardless of the fact that her body craved his like it did air and water.

"Never mind," she said. "Forget I—"

"The walls are coming down, Lilly."

The darkly murmured statement made her mind stutter to a halt. "What walls?"

"The ones between heaven, hell, and Earth. The walls that separate the hallowed from the cursed. That keep all the monsters in hell's bowels contained." He stood and walked over to the fireplace. For a moment, he stared at the glowing embers before he bent to add more wood.

"Every day, more and more creatures from the Beyond find their way. Slipping through cracks, easing through doors that shouldn't even exist. You want to know how hellhounds made it to your backyard? That's how. And it's not just them. Demons. Seers. Beings you can't even fathom. If humans were to find out what's happening, there'd be chaos."

"There's already chaos, Alex. Maybe you can't see it from up there"—she waved her hand in the air— "wherever the Beyond is, but there's plenty of chaos. Humans are a mess."

"Not like this. My world is about to implode, and when it does . . . I fear for you. I fear for all of God's creations."

"Why is it going to implode? What's wrong with it?"

"You mean aside from the demons?"

"Well, haven't they always been there? What's changed?"

He thought for a moment before answering. Alex didn't seem to be a man who spoke without consideration. Sometimes she could almost see him censoring his words, omitting and revising as he went. But right now he just seemed to be searching for the *right* words, not the safe ones.

"The Beyond has become a dumping ground. Your filth. Our filth. So many condemned and unredeemable souls. There's no safety valve. No way to release the pressure or dispose of the overflow. There's not room for anything else. Not anymore."

"What about God?" she asked. "You said he created the Beyond. Surely He watches over you."

"God has you. Why would he care about the trash?"

She swallowed hard, hating the pain she heard in those words, pain that echoed in *her* soul. That's how she'd felt when she'd learned that her own mother had abandoned her—discarded her like trash when she was too young to fend for herself.

He seemed to realize how much he'd revealed. Frowning, he turned away. "All I know," he said abruptly, "is that something happened in the Beyond and it was big enough to start the fires of Abaddon burning and open the door to Abaddon's prison. Now, there's a war brewing, and it's going to be ugly. If it erupts, it will bring an apocalypse that might destroy us all."

CHAPTER EIGHT

AFTER DROPPING THAT bomb, Alex said no more. He pulled on his coat and laced his boots, then went outside. Probably hoping to escape any other questions she might have queued up. Reluctantly, she let him go. She needed to process everything anyway.

While he patrolled the grounds of the cabin, she tidied up inside, at last storing some of Amy's things in cabinets and draws, grieving anew as she stuffed her sister's slippers in the back of the closet.

She was deep in thought when she heard the front door open and close again. Alex must have come back in. Feeling so vulnerable she could hardly stand it, she made the bed before going out to face him.

"All clear?" she asked.

"For now."

Her emotions were still strung tight, and clearly, so were his. Too many unanswered questions still circled between them. Like, *Does the apocalypse mean the same thing in your world as it does in mine?* And, what did "opened the door to Abaddon's prison" mean? What war was brewing? Against what enemy? And where did humans fit in?

But the question that rose to the surface inside Lilly, the one demanding an immediate answer, was much smaller . . . and at the same time, so much larger. It was Alex's world he spoke of—the place he called *home.* How did all of this mayhem affect *him?*

She stood across the room from him, wanting to blurt the question but sensing the barriers he'd erected while outside. His nonanswers would only hurt. Instead of pushing him again, she went to the closet and took down a puzzle she'd seen on the top shelf. It was a ploy her adoptive father had used when something troubled Lilly. Putting the pieces together often helped her organize her thoughts and talk about them. She had no idea if it would work on Alex, but it wasn't like they had a million other things to keep them busy.

"What are you doing?" he asked.

"We're stuck here for who knows how long. I'm going to go stir crazy if I don't do something."

He glanced from the puzzle box to her face.

"Unless you want to talk some more?"

He took the box and put it on the coffee table. Together, they went through the pieces of the puzzle, turning them face up, searching for the edges. The puzzle was a Christmas scene, complete with Santa flying over a small, festively decorated town.

They were silent for a long time before slowly, hesitantly, they began to exchange words with pieces. *Is that a corner?* or *I think that's part of the clock.* Before long, Lilly found herself telling him about her childhood, the parents who'd taken her in and made her theirs, and how the only father she'd ever known had loved puzzles and games.

"And laughing," she said. "I've never met anyone who found as much to laugh about as he did."

It made her smile just thinking of it now. Alex glanced up, smiled with her and went back to sorting puzzle pieces as she spoke, keeping that penetrating gaze on the table. But she could feel how closely he was listening.

"My adoptive parents were nothing like my birth mom. I don't think she even knew how to smile."

She fell into melancholy silence for a while. Alex looked up again.

"Keep talking. I like listening to you."

"It's your turn, now. Tell me something about you."

"I told you everything I can."

"I don't mean about the Beyond. I mean about *you*. What's it like for you, Alex? Living in this world of in-between . . . How do you fit in? It doesn't sound like a very nice place."

She tried to hide it, but even she heard the sympathy in her voice. He stiffened, his fingers curling into his palms and his muscles tightening—all defensive reactions. But he couldn't defend himself against the feelings she'd stirred with that simple question, and they both knew it.

"I don't need to fit in," he said coolly.

"Everyone needs that to some degree."

"I'm different."

"Different from what, Alex? Humans? Because from where I stand, not so much."

That brought his gaze to hers. The greens and golds glimmered with turmoil. He opened his mouth to say something, stopped, and tried again. "You don't know what you're talking about."

"True," she said, still watching him. Waiting. Because emotion moved across his face, so raw she felt the sting of it. Still, she couldn't decipher its source.

"I am meant to look like a human," he said.

"So you keep telling me. Are you meant to feel like one, too?" At his narrowed look, she clarified. "Inside. Emotions. *Feelings.*"

"No."

She sensed him waiting anxiously for what she'd say next, wariness in his every breath. She'd prodded at a sensitive spot he obviously didn't want exposed, yet she felt driven to pry at whatever he was hiding there.

"But you do," she said in a low, insistent voice. "Feel."

He tried to dismiss her with a headshake, but he only made it so far before the gesture died. He stood suddenly. Agitated. Lilly rose, too, while Alex watched her with a bated tension that trilled along her nerves. She moved closer until she was right in front of him, her head tipped back so she could stare into his face.

"You feel me," she said.

His eyes blazed as he lifted his hand and placed it over her heart. "Yes," he said, in case she didn't understand. "I feel you." He laughed softly. "I can't seem to stop feeling you."

It took all her willpower not to smile. Not to cheer. His hand slid up to the ridges of her collarbone, then to the hollow at the base of her throat. She wanted to lean into him, to put her hands all over him, too. Instead, she stood as still as he, waiting. Wondering what came next.

"Where I'm from . . . It's hard to describe," he said in a husky voice. "It's segregated. There are places inside the Beyond that even I don't know about. Our experiences are different, depending on what we are. Some creatures are trapped forever like caged animals. Some can move back and forth between the walls. Some can enter your world at will. It depends on what they are and what purpose they serve. Does that make sense?"

She nodded, but really, she wasn't sure she followed. He spoke of a place so ethereal that it was hard to put parameters around it in her mind.

"I'm a soldier. My purpose is to protect the secrets of the Beyond. It's critical that I fit in, here on Earth. That no one suspect I'm not one of you. I have to know how to talk, how to dress, how to speak. For that to happen, my world has to be based on yours. It's like a reflection. Everything we have, everything we are—it's an interpretation of you."

He paused, watching her watch him. The air seemed suddenly thin, the banked fire overly hot. Alex leaned closer, his fingers circling her throat in a gentle caress.

"We look like you. We talk like you. We think like you. But we aren't supposed to feel. We aren't supposed to *be* you."

"Why not?" she breathed, determined to prove him wrong.

"It isn't possible. We are *not* you."

"How do you know?" she insisted.

He glared at her, looking for a trap in her question. Maybe he had a right, because Lilly meant to corner him. She wanted him to see things from her perspective. Whether he liked it or not.

"I mean, you seem pretty human to me, Alex."

"I told you—"

"It's intentional. Yeah, I got it the first time. But what if it's more than that?"

Gently he circled her throat with his fingers, thumbs meeting in the middle. Lilly swayed into him, and he bent closer. A soft breath left her lips and fires began to burn in those intoxicating eyes. They flashed like Louisiana waters in summer heat, and all hope of self-control vanished in the steam.

"What if it's more than simply the way you look and act that's like us?" she asked. "What if you're exactly like us . . . you just don't know it?"

What if you can stay here?

The warmth of his breath fanned her cheek. The scent of his skin wrapped around her and made her long for more.

He shook his head and her heart thumped with painful regret, but then he spoke and his words stirred a crazy hope deep inside.

"There are rumors about a reaper who crossed over and survived. I don't know if they're true."

"By survived, you mean he's here? Living here as a human?"

"If gossip can be believed."

The possibility that Alex could stay, too, rolled over her.

He caught her stare. Trapped it, really, because once he made contact, there was no breaking free. The force of his masculinity surrounded her. He wasn't even *doing* anything and she felt it pulling her in.

His answer hung between them, an unspoken denial or confirmation, Lilly didn't know. He lowered his lashes, hiding his thoughts.

"Your skin is so soft," he said, brushing the back of his knuckles against her jaw before he cupped it, his hands hot against her face.

A mix of frustration and lust filled Lilly. She didn't want to allow him to distract her away from their conversation, but this wasn't something she could force. Only Alex could decide if he was willing to stay. Only Alex knew if he even wanted to try.

And only Alex could determine if what he felt for her was worth the risk.

His gaze dropped to her mouth and everything else got lost in his soft exhalation. He was going to kiss her and if he did, she knew she'd be lost. But did she move away? Did she avert her eyes or turn her head? Not even a little.

She met him in a kiss she craved in the deepest shadows of her soul. His lips were cold, his mouth hot. He tasted elemental. Copper, salt, desire . . . man. Her body didn't care if he was from the Beyond or Kansas. Millions of years of evolution drove her to him. In some primitive way, he tasted of her future.

A distant, alien sound broke the heated, sensual silence. Lilly and Alex pulled apart, both lifting their heads. His eyes closed as the strange baying—or *howling?* Lilly wasn't sure what it was—cut through the storm and settled around them. It brought a stroke of fear that traveled down her spine and heralded the reality Lilly didn't want to face. Even Belle bounded from her bed beside the hearth, barking loudly as she raced to the door. Lilly rested her head against Alex's chest, took a deep breath, and prepared to face whatever came next.

CHAPTER NINE

BELLE BARKED AGAIN, loud and insistent. Alex wanted to shout at the dog to stay quiet and praise the intelligent creature for sounding an alarm that the other animals soon picked up. Still, it took strength to step away from the soft curves and seduction of Lilly Winslow, and longer than it should have for Alex to convince himself he possessed the power to do it. She'd crumbled his defenses, leaving him exposed and out of his depth.

Who cared if others from the Beyond had hunted him down? Who cared if the whole fucking pack of hellhounds waited on the other side of the door?

Reluctantly, he acknowledged that he did.

He'd already killed once to protect Lilly. He'd do it again if he had to.

Another long bay echoed outside, and Lilly's dog pack rushed the door. All but the little one, Harley. The toy dog had been snoozing on the big chair, and in his attempt to join the excitement, he got tangled in the blanket and fell to the floor with an indignant yelp that got lost in the clamor. Another howl sliced through Alex.

"What's making that sound?" Lilly asked.

Alex's eyes widened as he stared into her face. "You heard it?" He strode to the window and looked out, afraid of her answer. "Tell me what it sounded like."

Lilly frowned. "A howl, but not like a wolf or coyote. Like something being tortured. What was it?"

"Did you hear it before?" At her bewildered expression, he clarified. "Before you found me fighting off the hellhounds yesterday."

"No."

"It's the bay of a hellhound, Lilly. Something you shouldn't be able to hear."

She paled as another eerie voice joined the first.

Alex's machete hung in its scabbard from a hook by the front door. Lilly's rifle rested against the wall nearby. They armed themselves quickly. Silently. Not touching, not even glancing at one another. Alex didn't dare look at her. It would only take one lingering look from her lovely eyes to distract him.

The dogs gathered in front of the door in an uproar, as if their combined voices might magically open it. Harley now danced between the other dogs' legs. Lilly picked him up a moment before Belle nearly trampled him, and Alex gave the big dog a disquieted glance. He hadn't forgotten how Belle had charged the hellhound attackers and brought one of them back to the pack.

"I'm worried about your dog," he said, pointing to the Great Dane.

"Belle?"

He nodded, lifting the edge of the curtain and peering out before he explained. Snow obliterated the sky, the earth, and the air in the middle. It fell in droves that drifted and whisked, banking against the cabin. It weighted tree branches and obscured the road down below. Lilly's SUV looked like a white lump beside the porch. Even the footprints he'd left earlier had long since been filled in or blown away. He listened for more baying, but only disturbing silence settled in with the cold.

He shifted, looking for new tracks or flashes of black against the snow . . . white lantern eyes glowing with malevolence. Nothing moved out there but the wash of white.

"Yesterday when the hellhounds had me pinned," he said, still scanning, "Belle attacked one of them about a second before it ripped out my throat. She chased it into the woods."

Lilly moved to his side and touched his arm. He faced her, taking in her drawn features and worried eyes.

"I saw that," she said. "I just didn't know what was happening. It looked like she slammed into an invisible wall when she was jumping over you. Then she ran off . . ."

"She chased it away." He frowned, still holding her gaze. "Hellhounds don't run from anything. But she chased one into the trees."

They both looked at Belle. The dog prowled back and forth in front of the door, but now stopped and stared back. She pricked her ears and cocked her head, as if listening to every word. The other dogs quieted and waited for the outcome of the conversation.

Uneasy, Alex went on. "Later, after you showed up and started shooting, she came back."

Lilly nodded. "Yes. I was so relieved. I'd just hiked halfway up that stupid mountain looking for her. I thought she'd run off again."

"But she wasn't alone," he said. "There was so much going on, I couldn't be sure of what I saw. But now . . . Lilly, she brought on of the hellhounds back with her. Like they were . . . friends. And it stood in front of you and didn't try to eat you."

"It was standing in front of *me*?"

He nodded. "And all the other dogs. They should have been tasty little treats to a hellhound. Especially that one."

He pointed at Harley. Ferociously, the Pomeranian growled back.

"What did the hellhound want?" Lilly said, frowning.

Alex gave a short, dry laugh. "Want? Usually blood. But that one . . . You'll have to ask Belle. She seemed to be communicating with it."

Lilly gave the big dog a stunned look. Belle opened her huge mouth and her tongue lolled out. Excitement over and escape denied, the other dogs padded away from the door and back to their beds by the fire. Alex certainly couldn't see any sign of trouble outside anymore. The baying—which Lilly had *heard*—had come from far off and, luckily, seemed to stay there.

Yet it had spooked the animals. It had spooked him, too. He'd fallen into a sense of false security, cocooned in this world of white with Lilly.

"How long has Belle been running off for that trail?"

"Since Amy died. Maybe before. I don't know."

Again, the pain lanced through Lilly's voice. He wanted to ask about her sister. Had they resembled one another? How had she died?

He wanted to touch Lilly. To pull her close and chase away the grief that shadowed her eyes. He wanted to find a quiet room and bang his head against the wall until his brain reengaged. This woman was not his.

"Keep talking," he said as he made one more round of all the windows. Each one gave him the same view. Storm. Snow. Silence.

"She always ran off in the mornings. About the same time every day. She'd come back before noon and I thought . . . I thought she was grieving. She'd spend the rest of her day wandering the house and yard . . . looking for Amy."

The sadness in her tone tugged at something inside him. He knew there were human customs that went with death, words that should be spoken and sentiments that should be shared. But he didn't know how to say what needed to be said, so he didn't try.

"You never noticed anything strange about her when she came back?" he asked softly.

Lilly shook her head, her eyes a mirror of her hurt and confusion.

And awareness. Even now, it hummed between them, that current that connected them while somehow keeping them apart.

Alex hung his machete by the door, then took Lilly's rifle from her unresisting fingers and propped it against the wall.

"I don't know jack about dogs," she said. "I keep thinking it should be easy, but apparently, I'm ill equipped. I'm probably doing everything wrong."

She gave a small, broken laugh and shook her head.

"I didn't even know I had a sister until last year. I didn't remember Amy, but she remembered me . . . remembered our mom giving me away when I was little. She'd been searching for me ever since she was old enough to do it. She finally found me. But only long enough to break my heart." Lilly sniffed and gave him a brave smile, the one that hid what she was really thinking. The one he was learning to hate.

"I'm sorry," he murmured.

She shrugged and looked away.

"Don't do that," he said. "Don't belittle it."

Her eyes had a glassy sheen when she looked back at him and tears hovered on her lashes. But her chin was tilted up and she didn't give him the chance to reach out to her.

"It is what it is," she said.

"Doesn't make it fair," he answered.

The brittle smile flashed again. "Fair? What do you know of fair? I was the lucky one. I got dropped off. Amy's life was hell with our junkie mother."

"Where did your mother leave you?"

Lilly cleared her throat, moved to the kitchen, and poured herself a glass of water as though it was the most important task in the world.

"Fire station," she said, her voice shaky.

She drank down her water then put the glass in the sink. It took her a few false starts before she went on.

"She left me in a box at the front door in the middle of the night. No note. Nothing to say when I was born or what my name was. Just me, a blanket and a dirty diaper. I was adopted before I turned one. Like I said, I was the lucky one."

He leaned against the counter beside her. "But?"

She ignored him until Alex took her hand and pulled her around to face him.

"But?"

She glared at the buttons on his shirt, and he thought maybe she'd continue to ignore him. Then she hung her head in defeat. "But my adopted parents died, too. And I was all alone. Again."

"How'd they die?"

"Someone broke into their house and robbed them. They woke up when it was happening and the robbers killed them both. Then they set the house on fire."

"Where were you?"

"A sleepover. I didn't find out until the next morning." She wiped her eyes. "I was a teenager—too old for another adoption. Not that I wanted one. No one could ever replace my parents. I figured out to make it in foster care for the time I had left, and once I was old enough, I figured out how to survive on my own." Her voice grew very soft as she spoke. She drew in a deep breath and squared her shoulders. Back to making herself look big to her enemy. Only in this case, she was her own enemy.

She didn't look at him, so Alex tilted her face back up until she had no choice but to meet his eyes. He didn't speak, but he waited until she did.

Lilly sighed. "Then Amy found me, and we had two months together before cancer took her, too."

Her voice cracked and the tears she'd tried to hold back welled and spilled. Angrily, she wiped them away. "And then . . ." she said, waving a hand between them.

She seemed to expect him to fill in the blanks, but he didn't know what came after *And then* . . . Nor did he understand the hurt and disappointment in her eyes when she realized it.

"Forget it," she muttered.

"No," he said, trying to figure her out. "And then . . . what?"

She jerked away from him and moved to the other side of the kitchen. But Alex didn't let her go far. He followed, crowding her against the counter, bracketing her with his arms, her back to his chest.

"And then, what?" he said in her ear.

"And then *you*, Alex," she answered stiffly, not turning around. "You crashed into my life and made me see—" She took a deep breath and shook her head. "You made me see how long I've been waiting for someone like you. And now you're here and you're just going to leave . . ."

The hollow silence that followed felt so big that Alex thought it might swallow him whole. How did he fill it? What did he fill it with?

He turned Lilly around in his arms and cupped her face with his hands.

"I can't change what I am, Lilly," he said softly.

"You don't know even know what you are," she shot back. "You said it yourself. You think you're a reflection. I think you're a man. You came to kill the hellhounds. After this storm passes, you'll go out and try again. You'll either succeed and go home or you'll die and go on to the afterlife. No room for me in either scenario."

She hadn't meant to say the last part. The resentful glitter in her eyes told him that. She didn't try to hide it from him, though. She stared him down, clearly wanting him to deny the truth she'd spoken. He could feel how bad she wanted it. But he couldn't lie to her.

"I don't have a choice," he answered, frustrated with her refusal to see that. "I can't leave them here, Lilly. They're killers. You saw what they did to Caleb."

"Okay. I get that. But after? Why do you have to leave? Why do you want to go back to something that isn't real? Or something that's *after* life. Why not stay here in *this* life?"

With me. She didn't have to say it.

Lilly took his hand between hers. "I'm real, Alex. This thing between us . . . it's real. I know it happened all fast. I don't know where it will lead. What it will make us. In two weeks, we might hate each other. But I want the chance to find out. I want *you* to want the chance, too."

Inside him, something caved, leaving a void for her words to fill.

He wanted that, too.

"I'm not afraid of being alone," Lilly said, staring at him with shining eyes. "I've learned to take care of myself. I've learned to move on. But I've also learned how short life can be. I don't like regrets. I don't want you to be one of mine."

With that said, Lilly went to the bedroom, closing the door behind her, leaving her standing there alone. Everything she'd told him resonated deep inside. She was right. If he left, he'd regret it. But if he stayed, he might bring evil to her front door, and he would regret that even more.

Chapter Ten

It was hours later when Lilly returned to the living room. Alex sensed her before he saw her. It seemed he had an antenna where she was concerned. Or maybe it was her sweet scent that alerted him, intoxicated him.

She'd showered, changed, and avoided him for most of the afternoon. He knew she wanted answers. She wanted some kind of agreement, if not full-fledged commitment. But Lilly wasn't willing to accept the truth.

Creatures of the Beyond did not belong in her world. Ever. The ones that tried broke the natural order of things. Who knew what damage they might eventually cause?

Alex stood by the fireplace, watching with guarded eyes as she wandered around the cabin, dogs at her heels. She might feel ill equipped to deal with her pack, but the dogs had obviously accepted her completely. They followed her like a parade, devotion in every step. All but Belle, who sat by the door expectantly. Alex stared at her, and she stared back with more intelligence than a four-legged creature should have.

Could it be possible that she'd made *friends* with a hellhound?

"Belle," Alex said. "Come."

She let him wait a moment before heeding his command. He quickly glanced at Lilly, who watched with indignant surprise. Devoted or not, the dogs never jumped to obey her. They only worshiped the ground she walked on. He understood.

The giant dog padded over to him and he knelt beside her. Belle let him stroke her head and along her back. She gave a soft whimper when he touched her belly. Frowning, Alex smoothed his palm over it again, feeling the hard heat there. Belle snuffled his ear as he gently probed.

After a moment, he looked up.

"What?" Lilly asked, coming closer.

He reached up and tugged her hand down toward Belle. Lilly crouched beside him and let him guide her fingers over the dog's abdomen. Something inside squirmed, something else shifted. He could almost feel the hard little heads and pointed elbows. Searching noses. Sealed eyes.

"Is that . . . Are those . . . *puppies?*"

"You didn't know?"

"It's not possible. Amy told me all the dogs were fixed—spayed, neutered. I can't remember which one."

He raised his brows. "Spayed for females. Neutered for males."

"*You* know?"

"Every male knows."

"How can she be having puppies if she's been spayed?" Lilly demanded.

"Your guess is as good as mine. Has she been around any male dogs?"

"Harley, but he's fixed, too."

They both looked at the little Pomeranian. Even if he'd been capable, there was no way he'd ever manage to impregnate the huge Dane.

"I never even . . . Amy was adamant about that. She rescued dogs. She wouldn't have had one in the house that hadn't been fixed. Too many unwanted animals in the world as it was, she'd say." Lilly stared at Belle with anxious eyes. "I can barely take care of the dogs I have. What am I going to do with puppies? Love them, of course, but five dogs is already too many."

He wanted to say he'd help her. He wanted it to be true.

Belle whined and moved to the door.

"She needs to go outside," Lilly said.

"I'll take her," Alex answered. "We're getting low on wood. Is there a stack somewhere?"

"By the shed. I'll come, too."

"I don't need help."

"Of course not. You only had a hellhound try to eat you yesterday."

She pulled on her coat and stuffed her feet into her boots while he did the same. He took her hat before she could reach for it and gently pulled it over her head. Hands still on the yarn cuff, he kissed her. Slowly.

Her lips parted, giving him access to the mystery of Lilly. He deepened the kiss, but he didn't touch her anywhere else. Just his fingertips on her hat and his lips against hers. Still, he felt her kiss in places that hungered for her.

Silently, he moved away and opened the door. The blast of frosty air cleared his head but it couldn't begin to cool his blood. Lilly followed him out. The sun hovered low on the horizon, gathering deep shadows as it crept away, but the last rays shone valiantly bright. They silhouetted her in gray and evergreen. Once again, she stole his breath.

"The shed's over there," she said, unaware of what she was doing to him as she pointed to the edge of the porch. The shed was a couple hundred feet to the left, but the blizzard obscured it. Even the trees had become mere smudges in a fury of white.

The dogs followed them out and scurried to their spots to do their business. When finished, they frolicked in the snow while Lilly and Alex moved wood from the side of the shed to the porch. They passed each other like dancers in a strange waltz, exchanging awkward glances and spare words as they worked. The snow muffled all sound, but the dogs seemed at ease and Alex let down his guard, just a little.

"Were you angry?" Lilly asked as they passed. She posed the question casually, as if in response to something they'd been discussing all along.

Alex's brow furrowed in confusion. "When?"

"You said God didn't care for his trash," she answered. "That your world was a dumping ground. You're an orphan, just like me."

She kept walking to and from the woodpile and squatted down to load up again, unaware of the impact of her question. Was he angry? Did he feel abandoned by his father? His creator?

He'd never thought of it before, or perhaps he'd always had it in his mind but simply ignored it, let it fester like the wound it was.

Lilly stood, arms filled with wood, and started back to the porch. When she saw him rooted to the same place, she slowed her steps.

Their eyes met in a moment of awareness . . . of her . . . of him . . . of the idea that they shared something as fundamental as common ground. Orphans. The both of them. Abandoned, yet surviving against the odds.

Lilly didn't indulge in self-pity, but she also didn't hide from the hurt that made her who she was. She took strength from the very things that reduced most humans to rubble. And she made Alex want to do the same. He felt a startling smile spread across his face. A smile that Lilly answered. In that strange and giddy moment, he felt understood.

He was falling—into Lilly's beautiful eyes, into her soft voice and hard truths. Since she'd challenged him in the woods with her rifle and dogs, he'd been spinning. Since she'd asked him how and why, he'd been caught in the storm of doubt. Since she'd made him think he was better than he really was, he'd been swept away in the tide of hope.

When he spoke, his voice was low and thick with emotion. "However this ends, Lilly Winslow, I'm glad I had a chance to be with you. You should know that."

Without hesitation, she dumped the wood she carried and threw her arms around him. Alex caught her against him and kissed her cold mouth, filled with sudden, indescribable happiness.

"The first time I saw you," she breathed, "I knew you were trouble. But I knew you'd be worth it, too."

"You should have run away."

"I'm glad I didn't."

As was he. He kissed her again, and she pressed closer.

"What did you think the first time you saw me?"

"That you had pretty eyes and I hoped I wouldn't have to kill you."

She met his gaze, dark humor mixing into the shining blue. "You wouldn't hurt me."

"I'm hurting you now," he murmured.

***

ALEX'S WORDS WASHED over Lilly. Sad and true, but somehow irrelevant. She didn't care if he hurt her as long as he touched her again. As long as he proved that their meeting, which had changed her in some deep, irrevocable way, had altered him, as well.

Suddenly, Belle lifted her head and woofed. Alex spun, staring into the distance.

"What is it?" Lilly asked as she searched the snowy landscape. "Did you hear something?"

Alex shook his head, but he continued to scan the dark woods around them. Lilly bent to retrieve the split logs she'd dropped and caught a shadow out of the corner of her eye. She looked up and froze.

Something stood a few feet in front of her. Dark as pitch and nebulous as a ghost, the creature had four legs and eyes so pale they glowed. Its outline shivered in and out of focus, making her think it was an illusion—a trick of frosted snow and afternoon gloom. Without a sound, it turned its back and faded away.

"Alex—"

His name caught in her throat. He'd moved closer to the shed and didn't hear her.

She searched for the creature—specter, whatever it was—and saw it again on the porch. Huge, but strangely insubstantial, textured like velvet. Belle bounded up the steps and padded to the beast's side. She bumped her head against its flank affectionately, tail wagging. A tongue came out from the black face and licked her.

"Alex."

This time he heard the panicked whisper. He spun and faced Lilly. He followed her fixed stare to the porch.

The creature faded again, but Lilly knew it was still there. Belle's tail wagged happily and she made soft sounds as she circled the space where the thing had been, her head down in deference to the apparition that Lilly knew must be a hellhound.

"You see it?" he asked, his voice as soft as hers had been.

"I see something," she clarified, unable to describe the pulsing silhouette that moved like a phantom.

In the distance, a sound rose up over the wind and wailed a piercing note that sent chills through her already ice-covered senses. Far to the south, another voice joined it, violent and hostile. Soon the shrieking howls surrounded them—nothing like the mournful wail of a wolf or coyote. The other dogs shifted in agitation, but they didn't bark. Instinct must be telling them that making a sound now would lead danger to their door.

"Get your gun," he murmured, chancing a look to where she'd leaned it beside the woodpile.

Quickly, she retrieved it and held it at the ready, scanning, searching, and landing on the Great Dane. Belle dashed down the stairs and herded the other dogs up to the porch. They shied to the right as they followed, and Lilly suspected the hellhound was still there even though she could no longer see it or hear it.

A tree nearby shuddered and suddenly Alex burst into action, swinging his blade and hacking at whatever had come at him. Lilly saw blurred shapes merging in the darkness and she fired, aiming for what she hoped were their massive heads. She picked off two of them while Alex cut down others like weeds.

A growl came from behind her, and she spun to find two dark creatures with blazing eyes and long, curved teeth standing there. She stumbled backward, trying to aim at the same time.

Then something launched itself from the porch. Belle's hellhound. It sank its teeth into the throat of the beast closest to her and shook, towing the bigger beast away from Lilly. The other turned in surprise, giving her a chance to aim and fire. Its head exploded and she looked away as fast as she could.

Frantic growls and yelps of pain came from nearby, followed by sudden silence. Belle's phantom hellhound solidified for a moment. It had blue eyes, she realized. As she took aim at its head, the creature stared at her with resignation Lilly couldn't mistake. The hellhound in her crosshairs braced itself, ready for the death sentence that Lilly had the power to give it.

But she couldn't pull the trigger. As horrendous and vicious as this killer might be, it had protected Belle . . . and it had protected Lilly.

She lowered her rifle.

"What are you doing?" Alex demanded, moving in front of her and raising his machete.

"No. No, Alex. Not that one."

"It's not a dog, Lilly. It doesn't belong here."

Lilly grabbed his arm, refusing to let him slaughter the creature. No, it didn't belong. It was an outcast, an outlier. Like Alex. Like Lilly. It had acted against its instincts or perhaps it had been driven by instinct older than the cursed body it inhabited.

It didn't belong, and yet . . .

"Maybe it can, Alex. If it's given a chance."

CHAPTER ELEVEN

THE HELLHOUND EYED Alex suspiciously as it backed away, then turned and dashed up the stairs onto the porch and rubbed its body down the length of the Great Dane's before it bounded over the railing and into the trees. Alex stared with his mouth open, unsure what to make of it. Of any of it.

He turned back, eyeing the hellhound bodies that littered the clearing. Six of them. When he'd seen them emerge from the shadows, his only thought had been to protect Lilly. She would not be ripped apart by them, not while Alex still had enough strength to lift his weapon. Not while he still breathed. He was shaking even now from the power of those emotions.

Exhausted and strangely wide-awake, he moved from one corpse to another. He put his blade through their hearts and sliced off their heads, even ones that Lilly had shot dead on. This time it wasn't luck that had guided her bullets. It was aim. She'd *seen* them. He didn't know how or why, but he knew it was true.

He finished his task as fast as possible. He'd burn the remains in the morning, but right now he just wanted to get Lilly and her crazy dogs into the cabin. Her face was pale, her blue coat splattered with hellhound blood. It hurt to think of the danger she'd been in.

When the door closed behind them, he pulled her tight against him.

"You could have been killed," he said, his voice breaking. Emotion he didn't understand washed over him.

"The hellhound . . . It protected me, Alex. Just like you do."

None of this made sense but Alex had seen the hellhound attack its own, too, just as Alex had when Jared had threatened Lilly. While Alex had battled the other hellhounds, the blue-eyed one had defended Lilly's dogs. And when the other hellhounds had cornered Lilly, it had saved her life.

He cupped her face and kissed her with his mouth open, putting all of his confusion, anger, and relief into the kiss. His other hand started on the fastenings of her coat, and her fingers were quickly there to help. He pulled back, watching as they both fumbled with the cumbersome buttons. Her eyes were heavy lidded, but they spoke. Those crazy, beautiful eyes. And he understood everything they said.

Her coat fell to the floor in a synthetic *swoosh*, and beneath it he found a beautiful woman with intriguing curves, soft breasts, and skin that felt like satin. For a moment, neither of them moved.

Nothing had changed and yet everything was different. For him. For her. Maybe forever. He thought he should say tell her, but his feelings overwhelmed him and he couldn't find the words he wanted to say.

"It doesn't matter," Lilly murmured against his skin. "Just this. Now."

She pulled off her shirt and Alex forgot everything else anyway. She stood in front of him in a simple white bra, her skin like alabaster in the dim light. Her pants rode low on her hips, below her belly. He gently touched the silky curve of her breast. The softness, the weight of it. It unhinged his mind and all thought fell into the emotional storm she created within him.

She unbuttoned his shirt and he shrugged out of it, pulling his undershirt over his head and dropping it to the floor. When she pressed against him again, skin to skin, he groaned.

Lilly took his hand, palm snug in his, and led him to the bedroom. So many things had changed since that morning. Grateful for another chance to be with Lilly, Alex made long, slow love to her, and he didn't even try to pretend it was anything less.

They dozed for a while after, holding each other in the cool shadows of the bedroom. There was no pulling away this time. No emotional withdrawal by either of them. They said very little, and yet Alex felt at peace. If he could have found a way to freeze the moment for eternity, he would have gladly committed to living them over and over again.

***

MUCH LATER, LILLY slipped from the bed and padded naked out to the kitchen. She returned after a minute wearing his flannel shirt and holding two glasses of water. Concern covered her face. "I don't know where Belle is."

Alex got up and helped her search. Belle wasn't on her bed or by the couch or the door. Lilly finally found her in the closet near the bedroom, circling as she tried to find a space to lie down, but the closet was too small for such a massive creature.

Lilly watched with bewilderment. "What does she want?"

Alex put his arm around her shoulders. "I don't know much about dogs, either, but most animals need to feel safe when they have their offspring."

Lilly looked at him, eyes wide as saucers. "She's having the puppies? *Now?*"

He shrugged. "That'd be my guess."

The cabin had few isolated places and none big enough for the Great Dane. At last, Lilly cleared their puzzle so Alex could turn the coffee table on its side. He pushed its legs up against a corner of the wall, creating a triangular box just large enough for Belle to stretch out. Lilly lined it with old towels, talking to Belle in a soothing voice as she coaxed her over. The corner was cozy and separate from the other dogs, and after a few apprehensive sniffs, Belle seemed to give it her approval.

Before the big dog could climb in, though, a loud thump came from outside and the other dogs began to bark again. More hellhounds? Dreading what she'd see, Lilly followed Alex to the window to look out. Two massive paws with long, jointed digits held on to the sill and a black head with blue eyes looked in.

Lilly recoiled, and Alex cursed softly. They both turned in surprise as Belle hobbled over to where they stood. The dog groaned as she went up on her hind legs, resting her paws on the windowsill. On the other side, the hellhound lowered its head and pressed its nose to the glass. Belle did the same.

"Are you seeing this?" Alex whispered.

Lilly nodded. She saw. She even understood in a strange and twisted way.

"Alex, what if that hellhound is the father?"

She knew he'd come to the same conclusion. There was no surprise in his eyes as he stared from one animal to the other. The hellhound made a low, whining sound, and Belle yipped in response before lowering her paws and making a slow, pained path to the enclosure they'd made for her.

Lilly turned away from the window and went to assist Belle. She brought Belle her water bowl and stroked her fur as she moaned through the start of her labor. Alex paced, moving from one window to another, watching for the hellhounds. Lilly knew he was worried that one of his fellow soldiers might have heard the gunshots from earlier and follow the sound to the cabin.

They should talk about that. About what he planned to do once the snow stopped coming down. But Lilly couldn't bring herself to broach the subject. She was afraid she might cry and beg this man, who was as much a stranger as a lover, to never leave her.

117

She knew it was ridiculous to feel so passionately about him. They'd only just met. Even if they could stay together, this feeling might not last. Yet Lilly couldn't make herself believe that it would ever go away. She didn't make instant connections with people, especially men. But from the moment he'd touched her on the trail, she'd been connected to Alex. He'd become a part of her, and she wanted the chance to know if he might become a permanent piece of her life.

"Lilly," he said, drawing her attention.

He was at the window that looked out on the porch. She came to his side, letting him pull her in front of him. His chest warmed her spine as he reached over her shoulder and pointed. On the rug by the door, the blue-eyed hellhound waited like a sphinx with his front paws crossed, head up, and ears pricked. She could see it clearly now. The phantom shadows had shivered away, leaving behind a solid form.

"You see it, don't you?" Alex asked.

She nodded. "I don't understand it, but yes. I see it. Clearly. Yesterday I couldn't see them or hear them at all. But now I can do both. Why?"

Alex shook his head. "I don't know."

She didn't say it but a theory had been forming while they'd worked on Belle's enclosure. It was vague, incomplete. Yet it resonated inside her and made her think.

"I've changed since you came here, Alex."

He gave her a sideways look, waiting.

"Knowing you, believing in the existence of your world, knowing how little time we have together . . . I've never been one to race headlong into a relationship."

She blushed and drew in a shaky breath. Was that what they had, the two of them? A relationship?

"I always guard myself. Make sure it's safe before I commit. But . . . from the moment when I looked into your eyes, I knew . . . I knew you were special. A broken heart would be worth what I might have with you. However short. However deep."

His eyes glimmered with understanding, and a gentle smile curved his lips. "I thought you looked like a soft, blue treat. I wanted a taste. I still do."

Tears pricked at her eyes, but she didn't let them go.

"Look outside, Alex. There's an evolution going on here. We just have to see it."

Confusion furrowed his brow, but he shifted his gaze to the window and looked at the blue-eyed hound standing vigil over a house of humans and dogs. Blue Eyes stared intensely back. Lilly took a deep breath and moved to the door.

"What are you doing?" he asked.

"Letting it in."

CHAPTER TWELVE

EVERYTHING INSIDE ALEX wanted to fight her logic. Let a hellhound live? Let it close to Lilly?

She'd opened the door before he could stop her . . . if that's what he'd even meant to do. Her words had worked like some dark and forbidden magic inside him. Evolution, she'd called it. He felt the truth of it down to his bones.

He'd lived his life as a reflection, seeing humans. Understanding their existence but never experiencing what it meant to feel, to care . . . to touch. And now that he had, he saw his world in a different way.

He'd believed that he didn't belong here. He'd broken laws by being with Lilly, by protecting her, by taking all of the sweetness she offered him. He'd thought those laws were sacred and to break them would somehow sully the world of humans, but Lilly believed differently.

She saw a place for him here. A place at her side, in her bed, in her heart. And more than anything, Alex wanted that place. He wanted that chance to belong. To her.

And here was this hellhound—*a fucking hellhound*—proving it could happen. A testament to the unpredictability of life right in front of his eyes. The hellhound stood and looked through the open door and into the cabin, with its cozy fire and fragile inhabitants.

Alex swore he knew what it was thinking. It wanted in, but it didn't feel worthy.

"Come on," Lilly coaxed.

It fixed those laser-bright eyes on her and tilted its head. Alex understood that, too.

Deranged female.

Alex moved to Lilly's side, took her hand, and echoed the invitation.

"Come."

At that, the hellhound stepped over the threshold, gave them another confused but grateful glance, and went straight to Belle. It jumped into her enclosure with lithe grace and lay down beside her, nose to nose. She licked its face and groaned softly.

Alex looked outside one last time before he closed the door. The snow didn't seem to be coming down as fast anymore. By morning, this storm would be over, but a new one had already begun . . . a storm of change, perhaps.

It took Belle hours to give birth to her three black puppies. Like the hellhound, they had big heads and long legs. Like their mother, they had velvety fur and ears. Alex wondered what their eyes would look like when they opened. Would they be pale blue or white lanterns? Or would they be chocolate brown like their mother's eyes?

"They're cute," Lilly announced, staring down at the ugly creatures with delight.

Alex laughed, but in a strange and probably completely wrong way . . . they were.

But all through Belle's long and arduous labor, Alex had heard hellhounds baying outside. With dawn, the next battle would come. One he might not win, but one he would fight with all his might. Because if he did survive, if he did destroy his enemy, he wouldn't be returning to the Beyond. He didn't care about the afterlife. He cared about *this* life that had been offered with no expectation that he would accept it.

He might not be worthy, but he wasn't an idiot, either. He would take it.

As the sun rose, Lilly put fresh blankets down for Belle and her new family. She brought water and food out for both the big dog and the hellhound. She fed Alex, too. He sat across the table from her, knowing he wanted to stay. Whether he belonged or not, maybe he'd never know. But if he could a find a way to make it happen, he would never leave. Yet the words wouldn't come, so he did the only thing he could—he made love to Lilly. He let Lilly make love to him.

The first time, they'd been driven by something primal. He still felt that. Lilly would always be a basic need in his life. Air. Food. Water. And Lilly. Not necessarily in that order. But as he let his fingers wander over her silken curves, what coursed through him came from deep inside. It was hunger and hope and belonging, all twisted into the spark that ignited when he moved between her legs and thrust into her body.

Nothing could compare to the feel of Lilly surrounding him, hot and wet and wanting. Him. Needing him to complete her.

In the end, he didn't say the words. But she knew.

CHAPTER THIRTEEN

BLUE SKY SHOWED through the clouds when Alex stepped from the bedroom. He went to the window to see what impact the bright sun had made on the frozen world. The sight that met his eyes stilled him. Shocked, he pulled Lilly beside him.

"Look out the window," he said softly.

Lilly's eyes widened as she took in the five hellhounds sitting on the porch, lined with military precision as they kept watch from every angle.

"I know this sounds crazy," he said, "but I think they're guarding us."

From somewhere nearby, the sound of more baying hellhounds raced across the bright morning. The hounds on the porch stood up, and Blue Eyes—as Lilly had dubbed him—jumped out of the enclosure. He gave Belle a parting glance that she seemed to understand. At the door, he turned those eyes on Alex.

The message was clear.

The battle was no longer coming. It was here, and these creatures of damnation were now his army, if Alex chose to lead them. He gave the hellhound a stunned laugh.

"Yeah. Okay."

The hellhound sneezed, shook its body, and waited for the door to be opened.

Alex strapped on his machete, and Lilly reached for her rifle. He hated the thought of her going out into what could only be a bloody fight. But she gave him a bright smile.

"I'm an even better shot when I can see what I'm shooting."

He laughed again. It was ridiculous to be so happy in the face of imminent violence. Yet he couldn't stop grinning at her. "Did you really learn to shoot from YouTube?"

She pressed her mouth to his. "Ask me tomorrow."

Her pack of crazy dogs gathered around the hellhound at the door, ready to accompany Lilly outside and fight at her side. Even the toy dog danced with impatience.

She told them all to sit this one out.

"Stay with Belle, girls."

Harley barked in protest, but when Lilly settled him beside Belle, he nudged the puppies into place and patrolled the edges of Belle's enclosure like a sergeant.

"Lilly," Alex said before he stepped outside.

"Don't you dare say good-bye."

Alex shook his head. "Not a chance. If we get out of this, only God himself can take you from me or me from you."

"It was always that way, Alex. Didn't you know it?"

He smiled again and kissed her, and together, they went out to fight for their future.

Chapter Fourteen

LILLY DIDN'T KNOW what to expect of the hellhounds who'd stood guard, but she had faith that they wouldn't turn on her and Alex when they stepped out. She was so focused on the interaction between the animals that she hadn't seen three men slip out of the trees until she heard Alex curse under his breath.

The hellhounds leaped over the railing and made themselves a front line for this new enemy. Lilly's mouth was dry as she watched the men warily approach. They each carried a weighted machete just like Alex's, walking side by side. They slowed as they passed the bloody circle where the hellhounds had fallen last night.

Finally, the three men stood in front of them. They eyed the hellhounds that defended Lilly and Alex with distrust. Who could blame them? Lilly glanced at Alex's face. He knew these men. Something twisted in her heart. If they attacked, which is what it looked like they intended to do, Alex would be forced to fight against his own again. And it would hurt him inside.

"What is this madness?" the man standing in the middle asked.

"Change, Jackson," Alex answered darkly. "This madness is change."

Jackson shifted his gaze from the hellhounds to Lilly and then to the way Alex held her hand in his. She saw something shine in Jackson's eyes. Astonishment, mixed with rejection.

"A human female?" Jackson demanded.

That was the first thing he asked? Lilly might have laughed if not for the loud baying that rushing them from all sides. The three men brought their weapons up, turning to stand with their backs to one another, making a ring with their bodies.

"Stay with me, Lilly," Alex said. "Back-to-back, like they're doing."

She barely had time to do as he instructed before the first hellhound broke from the trees. In seconds, more joined. A lot more. So many she lost count. The sounds of growls and breaking bones, of blood-curdling howls and pained screams filled the air. They fought without speaking. Lilly loaded and fired, but the hellhounds learned quickly that she could see them now and they dodged her shots with greater speed and more respect.

Blue Eyes, and the five hellhounds that had followed him, dove into the melee without hesitation. Blue Eyes worked in tandem with Lilly, wounding the ferocious creatures and slowing them down enough for her to shoot.

The battle might have lasted for days or it might have ended in seconds. Lilly had no frame of reference. She focused on the danger coming at her head-on and on

Alex behind her, still standing, still swinging. And then suddenly it was over.

Slain hellhounds covered the ground. The snow had become slushy, and now it mixed with blood and gore, sharp with the stench of sulfur and brutality. Of the three men, only Jackson still stood. The others lay in mangled pieces beside the black beastly corpses.

Shaking, Lilly lowered her rifle and tried to catch her breath. Blue Eyes and two of his mates gathered around her, and cautiously, she petted one, then another as they nudged forward for attention.

Jackson moved to Alex's side and watched Lilly with the animals. His jaw dropped and his eyes grew wide. "I don't understand this," he said.

From the corner of her eye, Lilly saw agreement on Alex's face. The turn of events didn't make sense to him, either. Yet with each passing moment, Lilly sensed that Alex's shock had waned and in its place was acceptance . . . tolerance . . . hope.

"It confuses the hell out of me, too," Alex said. "But it is what it is."

Jackson huffed. "And what the fuck is that?"

"Evolution?" Alex offered, meeting Lilly's eyes and smiling into them. "It's the wave of the future, my friend."

Jackson shook his head. "Your future, maybe. But not mine." He looked down at the bloody mess around them and the eviscerated bodies of his comrades. Silently, he and Alex moved through the maze of dead hellhounds, putting blades through hearts, removing heads. When finished, Jackson approached the hellhounds that had fought for Alex and Lilly.

They sat in a row, ever watchful. It seemed they'd prepared themselves to face whatever might come next, even death. Lilly was moved by their courage. She believed they'd earned a right to live, but the two men facing them might not agree.

"What do you want to do with them?" Jackson asked with a nod at the creatures.

"Let them live," Alex said, and Lilly wanted to cheer. "There are others still out there, waiting to attack. Maybe others that want to belong. Either way, we might need the backup later."

Jackson gave Alex a hard look. "It's not natural. You know how cunning they can be. They're playing a game, and once your guard is down, they'll turn on you."

There was a very real chance that Jackson could be right, but Lilly didn't believe it. She shifted her gaze to Alex.

"They've had plenty of chances to do their worst," he said. "Now they need a chance to do their best."

Jackson shook his head again. "Hellhounds on Earth. I hope you know what you're doing."

Alex smiled at Lilly. "Not a clue. But we'll figure it out. I'm where I need to be, though, and so are they."

A taut silence fell after those words, and Lilly felt her chest tighten with the tension that moved between Alex and Jackson.

"You're going to try to stay," Jackson said after a long moment.

"Yes."

"Even though it's forbidden."

"Yes."

Jackson's gaze lingered on the hellhounds sprawled at Lilly's feet before shifting to her face. She could see the questions in his eyes. He didn't understand how she'd convinced Alex to stay. He couldn't imagine why he'd be willing to risk everything for her.

"I won't lie for you," Jackson warned with a gruff sigh. "But I won't volunteer any information, either. I'll tell them I saw you in battle. I'll tell them I presume you dead—which I do, just so we're clear. They may be able to track you from the Beyond, though. You know that."

"I know they've claimed they have that power. But I've learned a lot since I came here. I've learned they lie."

Jackson seemed unsettled by this comment, but in the end, he didn't argue the point.

The two men embraced, and Alex said something to Jackson that Lilly couldn't hear. Jackson pulled back with a stunned laugh. He was still laughing as he walked away, disappearing into the trees. Leaving Alex behind. With her.

He'd chosen her.

Alex took her hand and led her up to the cabin. The hellhounds spread out and flopped down on the porch, clearly exhausted and no longer on watch. They felt safe. Against all odds, so did Lilly.

Blue Eyes followed them inside and joined his mate in the enclosure. Lilly watched as he licked his pups before settling down beside Belle. He let out a loud and contented sigh, and closed his eyes. Seeing that his work was done, Harley jumped out of the enclosure and went to snuggle with the other dogs on their beds by the fire.

"What did you say to Jackson?" Lilly asked.

"I told him that evolution had its perks."

"Meaning?"

"He knew what I meant."

Alex's smile warmed her from the top of her head right down to the soles of her feet.

"So, Lilly Winslow . . . Now that you've got me, what are you going to do with me?"

Lilly grinned back. "I'm pretty sure I'm going to fall in love with you, for starters."

"I like that plan," he said, lifting her off her feet and carrying her into the bedroom. "I'm pretty sure you won't be alone in it."

As Alex kissed her to prove his point, Lilly decided that she was very much going to enjoy this forbidden life of Alex Moore.

Other books by Erin Quinn

The Beyond Series

The Five Deaths of Roxanne Love (Book 1)

The Forbidden Life of Alex Moore (Novella 1.5)

The Three Fates of Ryan Love (Book 2)

The Seven Sins of Ruby Love (Book 3) 2015

The Mists of Ireland Series

Haunting Beauty (Book 1)

Haunting Warrior (Book 2)

Haunting Desire (Book 3)

Haunting Embrace (Book 4)

About the Author

Erin Quinn is a NYT bestselling author. Her books have been called "riveting," "brilliantly plotted" and "beautifully written" and have won, placed or showed in the Booksellers Best, WILLA Award for Historical fiction, the Orange Rose, Golden Quill, Best Books, and Award of Excellence.

She lives in Arizona with her husband, two daughters and three dogs (all of whom have made debuts in her stories—the dogs, that is, not the husband and kids.)

Erin Quinn loves to talk to readers. If you have a book club or reading group and would like to discuss one of her books, let her know! Please contact Erin for more information by using the contact form on her website. www.erinquinnbooks.com.

KEEP READING FOR A PREVIEW OF

THE THREE FATES OF RYAN LOVE

BOOK TWO IN THE BEYOND SERIES,
AVAILABLE NOW FROM POCKET BOOKS.

THE THREE FATES OF RYAN LOVE
ERIN QUINN

CHAPTER ONE

RYAN HEARD THE first of the sirens as he turned into the home stretch of his run. He ran most every night after he closed Love's, the bar he owned with his two sisters. The exercise usually cleared his mind, but not tonight. A storm had started brewing as he'd clocked the first mile and the kind of cold that was indigenous to the desert seeped beneath his skin and made old wounds ache. The glowering sky pressed down on him, sinister against the excessive Christmas lights twinkling merrily around every palm tree and the festive banners that snapped in the bitter wind. Instead of clearheaded, Ryan felt chased.

His German shepherd, Brandy, ran at his side, ears up and swiveling. Even she didn't seem to be enjoying the ritual as much as usual.

Glad when Love's came into sight, Ryan slowed his steps and tried to catch his breath. The sirens were closer now and a police car flew past to join more flashing lights about a block down the street. It was after two in the morning, but Mill Avenue near Arizona State University never really slept. Probably drunks out causing trouble. Maybe even the three he'd thrown out of Love's that night. They'd left him with a bruised face and sore ribs.

Watching through the spitting rain, Ryan cut across an alley and into the parking lot behind Love's. That's when he heard the woman scream.

He spun to face the nook between the south wall of Love's and the cinder-block barrier that hid the side door to the kitchen. He peered into the dark recess, sure that's where the sound had come from, but nothing moved. Brandy's ear swiveled as she barked, trying to sniff and see everything at once. She didn't seem able to pinpoint the scream either.

The next scream echoed around him at the same time pressure filled the space behind his ears and made him feel unbalanced. He stumbled back as lightning flashed and a tremendous bolt snapped down right in front of him. When he looked again, a woman sat inside the small, sheltered alcove with her knees pulled up and her arms wrapped around them. Seconds ago, only darkness had waited there. Long, dark hair gleamed under the muted light, spilling over her shoulders and hiding her face. Her skin had an alabaster sheen. There was a lot of it, too. He frowned. She was naked.

With a hand signal for Brandy to sit, Ryan wiped the rain from his face and approached her cautiously.

2

The walls and awning shielded her from the rain, but not the cold. She shivered violently as he crouched down in front of her.

"Hey," he said in a soft voice. "How'd you get here? Are you okay?"

She looked up with wide, clear eyes as blue as a desert sky. Even in the dark the color was vivid and they shimmered with something he couldn't begin to define. Long lashes the same rich shade as her hair framed them and accented their luminescent glow. They tilted at the corners, catlike. The dark wings of her brows drew focus to the shape of her face, the smooth line of her nose, the dusting of freckles that covered it.

He dropped his gaze and saw a raw scrape on her shin, another up high on her thigh. A third marred her shoulder. He thought of the sirens and police he'd heard. Was she involved in whatever had been happening?

"Ryan?" she whispered, chasing that thought right out of his head.

The sound of his name on her lips raised the hairs at the back of his neck, somehow trumping everything else. Like who she was, what she was doing here stark naked in the middle of the night.

"You know me?"

He peered into her face, sure he'd never seen her before.

"You're Ryan," she said with more certainty.

Her gaze shifted to something behind him. Ryan looked over his shoulder to find Brandy right at his heels with perked ears and a wet, wagging tail, watching the woman. The woman stared back at his dog with what Ryan would swear was wonder.

"Who are you?" he asked.

"Sabelle," she replied, still watching his dog.

Brandy got down on her belly, inching closer in the most unthreatening manner a ninety-five-pound German shepherd could manage.

"Where are your clothes, Sybil?"

She shook her head, pulling her gaze from Brandy to look him in the eye. "S'*belle*," she corrected. "Not Sybil."

"S'belle," he pronounced carefully. "Why are you naked?"

A hot flush turned her skin pink a second before she lied. "I don't remember."

She shifted with agitation and Brandy made a sound low in her throat. Not aggressive. Consoling. The dog had managed to army-crawl close enough to put her big fluffy head on the woman's lap. Sabelle's lips parted as she settled her fingers on Brandy's silky black ear.

She shivered and goose bumps rose on her skin. Ryan quickly reached over his head and pulled off his shirt. It was warm from his body, but damp from the rain. It would cover her, though.

"Here, put this on," he said, handing it over.

She accepted it, fingering the soft fabric before she pressed it to her face, smelling it. The action was so surprising that at first all he could think to do was mumble, "Sorry, it's all I have," while hot embarrassment flooded his face.

"It smells like you," she said.

Like it was a good thing.

His mouth opened but no words came out. He lowered his eyes while she pulled the shirt over her head. When he looked back, she was covered, thank God. His shirt was huge on her. The shoulders drooped to her elbows and the long sleeves hid her hands.

She huddled in it, her gaze roaming his face, lingering on the cut over his nose, the puffy skin on his cheek, and his swollen jaw. He almost felt the quicksilver stare on his bare chest and bruised ribs. He must look like a big ugly thug to her.

She had bruises and scrapes of her own. He could only hope that her wounds had come from something less violent than his.

"What happened to you? Did someone hurt you?" he asked.

"No," she said with a definitive shake of her head.

"You screamed."

"I didn't expect it to be painful."

"You didn't expect *what* to be painful?"

She flinched at his sharp tone. "Coming here."

He didn't know what to say to that. *Here*—in the parking lot in the middle of the night—wasn't anyplace she should be, but she'd obviously been hurt, was probably in shock. She might not even know where she was. He dug his phone out of his pocket and leaned in so the rain running down his back wouldn't get it wet as he dialed 911.

The storm picked up its pace, hitting the asphalt with such force that raindrops bounced and pooled, pounding the awning overhead with fury. Storms moved fast in Arizona, but this was insane.

"Who are you calling?" she asked.

"The police. They'll—"

She snatched the phone out of his hand and hit the screen repeatedly until the ring cut off.

Ryan's mouth was open again. "Okay, now it's getting weird."

"No police," she said. "What time is it?"

When he didn't answer immediately, she repeated the question sharply.

"I don't know. Two? Three in the morning?"

Her eyes rounded and she scrambled to get her feet under her. "We need to go. Now, Ryan."

She stood, long legs protruding from his big shirt. Her hair brushed her shoulders and impatiently she swiped it back. Standing as well, Ryan reached out to steady her as she swayed.

"Easy, girl," he murmured gently. "Slow down. Take a breath. You're safe now. Let's get the police here. They'll get everything worked out."

"No police," she insisted. "They can't help."

"Yeah, well. . . ." *Neither could he.* "Can I have my phone back?"

She turned and started out of the shelter.

"Wait," he said. "Sabelle Whoever-You-Are. Wait."

She seemed more alert, more focused, but she'd obviously hit her head. She tucked her arms tight, hands jammed under her pits and head bent as she gingerly picked her way through the glass, gravel, mud, and puddles covering the parking lot, ignoring him until she stepped on something sharp and gasped.

"Hold up. Would you stop?" he said, exasperated. "Let me help you."

He lifted her in his arms and carried her to the back door before she could protest. She wasn't a big woman, but she was lush with all the right curves in all the right places. She felt solid against his chest and soft in ways that played games with his traitorous thoughts and made him glad for the bracing rain. Brandy escorted them like a devoted admirer, her wet nose brushing Sabelle's feet whenever the dog could reach them. Ryan paused before opening the door, half convinced he was making a big mistake. This was the kind of thing you saw on the news where some dumb putz just trying to help ended up accused of wrongdoing.

He jockeyed her weight as he fumbled his keys from his pocket into the lock. Sabelle tightened her arms around him, pressing all those feminine curves closer as Ryan tried valiantly not to notice.

Darkness clustered just inside and obscured the stairs all the way up. The rain boomed against the roof and the cold made plumes of their breath. His skin felt icy.

Except where he held Sabelle. She was like a furnace heating his bare chest.

The door slammed shut behind them as Ryan hit the lights and set Sabelle on her feet again. She continued to hold onto him, staring into his face as if to memorize his features. For all her crazy talk, her eyes looked clear and focused in the dim glow.

Then she twisted away and started up the stairs to his apartment without asking or waiting for an invitation. With a muttered curse, Ryan started to follow but fingers of disquiet played down his spine, making him pause.

The area under the stairs to his apartment served as storage for cases of beer and other supplies. A door straight ahead made a convenient back entrance to the bar, just as the door behind him was a quick shortcut to the parking lot. Usually the stairwell smelled of cardboard, hops, and old french fries. Familiar, comfortable odors that lingered in most bars. Tonight a whiff of rotten eggs hung over it.

Sabelle was already at his front door, waiting. He'd figured out what smelled after he dealt with her. She tried the knob, found it unlocked, and let herself in before he made it up the stairs. Stunned by her audacity, he picked up his pace. Brandy raced ahead and was beside her as Sabelle padded past the kitchen breakfast bar, trailing fingers over the back of the couch as she took in her surroundings.

His apartment was a loft that stretched over Love's. One room with a wall of windows, it had a spacious, open feel that suited him. Her gaze lingered on the screen sectioning off his bedroom before moving to the clock on the microwave. The digital readout read 2:30. He saw her note it with a deep breath and a nod.

"There's still time." She faced him with determination. "I've come with a warning. Your life is in danger."

He might have smiled if she hadn't looked so distressed. "Okay," he said carefully.

She nodded, apparently satisfied with that response. "Good. I'd hoped you'd understand. We need to leave here." She glanced at the clock again. "Quickly."

"And go where?" he said, not understanding at all.

"Away from here. *Here* is where it happens."

Ryan studied her, suddenly weary to the bone. Ever since his brother's bizarre death—*Murder? Suicide?* Ryan doubted he'd ever know the truth—Love's had been a tourist attraction for lunatics. Fanatics who thought that Ryan's twin brother and sister were blessed by the heavens or cursed by demons had always been on the fringe of their lives. Reece and Roxanne had died (and miraculously been revived) more than once. It went with the territory.

Some of the crazies were dangerous, others merely curious. He didn't know which camp Sabelle fell into, but the sooner he got her out of here, the better.

"You don't believe me," Sabelle said with a hint of disappointment in her voice. "I don't know why I'm surprised. It's in your nature to be suspicious. You have trust issues."

Maybe so. But that was his business. "What's this danger I'm supposedly in?" he asked politely.

"Death," she replied almost eagerly. "Yours, I mean."

9

He let out a deep breath and shook his head. "Listen, Sabelle. I'd like to help you, get you someplace safe. How about back home?" *Or the psych ward you escaped from?*

"I can never go home," she said vehemently.

He lifted his hands, palms out. "Fair enough. But you can't stay here. I just pulled a twelve-hour shift. I'm tired. All I want is a hot shower and bed."

Her eyes widened and she shot another quick glance at the screen that hid his bed. Something darkly erotic flashed across her features. For a moment, he couldn't look away.

"I know you don't believe me," she said, her voice breathy and low, "but this isn't a game or a joke. You can't just take a shower and pretend it will go away. Do you think I would risk so much to warn you if there was nothing to fear?"

"I think you're a confused woman who needs some help."

"I'm not confused. An explosion will decimate this building sometime between now and three a.m. Your apartment will be incinerated. Boom. *Gone.*"

"Between now and three a.m.," he repeated, deadpan.

"Stop it. Stop pretending disbelief you don't feel."

"Oh, I feel it."

Narrowed eyes were the only clue that she'd heard him. She didn't argue, she didn't try to add details to support her claim. Most liars did.

"You'll need the money you have stashed beneath the floorboards in your bedroom," she said with a challenging glance. "Clothes, of course. And Brandy. We'll need her."

"We?"

"I don't know how much time we have, Ryan. I only know that by three, it will all be over. For both of us."

She was all-in when it came to this fantasy quest, and her conviction planted a seed of doubt that startled him.

"You are more important than you know, Ryan."

The laugh he'd tried for earlier finally emerged and his doubt waned. The poor woman was definitely delusional.

"I own a pub. Actually, I own about one-fiftieth of a pub. The bank owns the rest. I spend most of my days and nights behind a bar, serving drinks to people who have less of a life than I do. Unless it's critical that the drunks get their next drink, I'm the opposite of important."

With a superior sounding sniff, she moved behind the Japanese screen and into his bedroom. Dumbfounded, Ryan followed, watching her open his closet. She yanked his backpack off the top shelf and stuffed his favorite jeans, a T-shirt, and a flannel button-down into it.

As she turned, she caught her reflection in the dresser mirror and did a double take. For a moment, she stared at her pale face like she'd expected to see someone else looking back.

He tilted his head to the side, watching her watch herself. She saw the movement and quickly glanced away but her cheeks pinked up and she avoided looking at him. She began opening his drawers like she had every right.

And instead of throwing her out on her pretty little ass, he watched her, still trying to figure out what to do about her. Wrestle his phone away? Humor her back outside and lock the doors behind her?

The storm boomed so loud it shook the walls. He couldn't throw her out in this.

In his top drawer, she found his briefs, added a pair to the pack, and pulled open the next drawer. She rummaged until she retrieved some basketball shorts and held them up to her hips. When she tugged them on, she gave him an eyeful of long legs and bare behind.

She turned and busted him staring. His gaze snared hers and something darkened in the uncertain blue. Neither one of them looked away.

"Do you have shoes I could borrow?" she asked, her voice husky.

He pointed to the other closet door. It took her a moment to turn around and slide the door open. She eyed his size 14 shoes dubiously before she spotted a pair of flip flops on the floor and slipped her feet into them.

"Get the money, Ryan."

Crazy with sprinkles on top. That's what this was.

"You planning on robbing me?" he managed to say.

She faced him. "Is that what you think? Are you afraid I'm going to tackle you and steal all your precious belongings?"

She was swimming in his big shirt. The shorts hung down to her knees and the flip-flops looked like snowshoes on her feet. She had the threat potential of a puppy.

Again, he wished he could muster a laugh. Instead, "No" emerged in a wooden tone.

"Get your stuff and wait it out on the sidewalk with me, then. If nothing happens by three, you can call your police and wash your hands of me."

She handed him his phone like a gesture of good faith. He took it.

"Or I could do that now and save myself the trouble."

"Yes. You could do that. But we'd both pay the price for your stupidity."

"Did you just call me—"

"You are in *danger*," she said, enunciating each syllable sharply. "You're going to die if you don't trust me. How much clearer can I be? I know you're the kind of man who has to see something to believe it. But why not see it from the outside with me?"

With that, she grabbed his backpack and dropped it at his feet.

He still hadn't moved, but Sabelle didn't wait. She crossed to the front door with a stiff back and an air of determination, ridiculous in her borrowed getup and yet somehow . . . convincing.

"How would you know what kind of man I am?" he asked softly.

The question made her pause. She shot a guarded glance over her shoulder, eyes wide and lips parted. Bravado and hunger stared back at him, a combination so mystifying that it shut his mouth.

So what if she was right? It wouldn't be the strangest thing to have happened in the past month. Hell, in the last week. Even as common sense told him that it was more likely she had someone waiting downstairs to relieve him of the money she'd insisted he pack, he felt himself giving in.

She'd said *beneath the floorboards.* If she already knew where he kept the money, why not just break in and steal it while he'd been out for his run? Why the elaborate *naked-and-afraid* act?

"I see you thinking," she said. "You're deciding on all the reasons not to trust me. But that's wasting time you don't have. Look at the clock, Ryan." She paused. "*Please.*"

It was the hitch in her voice that unplugged his common sense and pushed him to the edge.

He exhaled a heavy breath. "Let me get a shirt."

The tremulous smile she couldn't hide fast enough called him a fool, but the baby-blues sent another coded message he couldn't be sure he'd read right. He ducked behind the screen that divided the rooms and pried up the floorboard by his bed with a long flathead screwdriver he kept in his nightstand drawer just for that purpose. He stuffed the whole hard-earned 10K into his backpack, shrugged on a shirt, and snagged jackets for both of them on his way out. What could it hurt to sit in his truck and wait it out? If nothing else, maybe he'd get to the bottom of her story.

She waited impatiently by the door, watching the clock switch numbers. Brandy sat at her feet, ready to go. According to Sabelle, they had less than fifteen minutes to get out of there before the whole place was incinerated.

"Hurry," she said and stepped onto the landing without a backward glance.

Shaking his head, Ryan clicked his tongue for Brandy to follow and locked the door behind him.

CHAPTER TWO

SABELLE FELT RYAN following her all the way down the stairs. Outside, the storm raged in vengeance and she tried not to pin more importance on it than it deserved. But it was hard. It could be a storm and it could be the Sisters. Knowing what they planned for Ryan, it seemed wise to consider the latter. The storm could be a symptom of their anger.

They would know she was gone by now.

When they reached the bottom of the stairs, Ryan paused, muttering, "Something smells rotten down here."

Sabelle got a whiff of the pungent odor, too, but her sense of smell was something new and the only scent that mattered to her was the warm, masculine one that clung to Ryan's jacket. She pressed her nose into the collar as he took her hand and the lead, turning right toward the pub instead of to the left and the parking lot where he'd found her.

His hand was warm against hers. She felt it from her fingertips to someplace low and deep inside her, a human reaction to his nearness that disconcerted and delighted her. She'd imagined it enough times, but she'd never considered the impact of *feeling*.

They entered the pub from a door behind the bar with Brandy racing ahead. A hundred times she'd seen Ryan's family pub through his eyes, but she'd never seen it through her own. She'd never imagined the *taste* of it. The air was thick and malty, sharp and sour all at once. The graying walls held memories of secrets shared by friends long gone. Framed pictures of Ryan's relatives posing with people she didn't know watched her pass, judging her from their lofty positions.

High up along the front wall, stained glass in brilliant emerald and dusty rose filtered the streetlights and danced pastels over the long smooth bar. Below them, hazy picture windows looked out on a deserted street where twinkling Christmas lights glimmered from every tree and pole she could see.

"It's smaller than I expected," she murmured.

Ryan gave her a questioning look but she didn't say more. The responsibility of the pub had always seemed such a huge burden for Ryan that she'd expected an echoing chamber instead of a cozy niche. Her steps faltered as she stared at the empty tables and chairs, knowing soon they'd be rubble and ash. Ryan tugged her hand.

"Did you forget we're about to be incinerated?"

Not something to joke about, but he'd figure that out on his own. Pack on his back, Ryan took a few steps toward the exit and stilled. He sniffed the air again.

"Fuck," he breathed. "That's gas."

His accusing gaze swiveled toward her. The fury of the storm amplified the silence inside the bar as the moment stretched. Hail began to pelt the walls and sidewalk. It battered the roof and bombarded the windows.

Ryan cursed again and moved to the door, her fingers firmly clasped in his. Sabelle matched his stride, suddenly worried that she'd gotten it wrong and they'd run out of time. He had the key in the lock and the door opened in seconds.

"Keep your head down," he said, shrugging out of the jacket he wore and holding it over them both. "Get closer."

Dutifully, she obeyed, wrapping her arm around his waist to anchor her to his side.

"Brandy, come," he ordered as they stepped onto the sidewalk. Brandy didn't look too keen on the idea, but she scooted out and stayed close.

"Good girl," he praised as the icy wet wind blasted into them.

Ryan didn't take the time to lock this door behind him. Filled with panic, Sabelle held on as they raced across the street, hail hammering them with vengeance. When they reached the shelter of the awning on the other side, Sabelle finally looked up.

Inside, Ryan's pub had seemed small, but outside on the street, the world felt endless.

Dark buildings stared vacantly down at the lights twinkling at street level. *Happy Holidays* banners flailed in the frigid onslaught. They passed in front of a bus stop with an advertisement pasted to its back wall of a hotel nestled in a cove of towering red rocks. Someone had spray-painted black eyeballs over it and signed *Wa Chu* beneath in an elaborate font. She noted it grimly.

Hail bounced against the street like clouded diamonds. Beside her, Ryan stood warm and strong.

This was really happening.

Ryan faced Love's with a look of foreboding on his face that she'd seen before. She knew that as a boy he'd held his finger against the leaking holes his mother's death had caused in the family. He had better methods as a man, but he was still patching the dyke with his very soul.

She couldn't stop looking at him. Couldn't keep her thoughts focused on anything but where he stood in relation to her. The rhythm of his breathing. His smell. He was the kind of man people depended on. The kind she hoped she could, too.

He pulled her into a recessed doorway, dug his phone out of his pocket, and punched in some numbers. While he listened, a hot breeze whisked around them, tugging at the hem of her shirt, tousling his hair. It felt so good in the icy cold that Sabelle faced its warmth.

A tinny voice answered Ryan's call. "Nine-one-one operator. What's your emergency?"

"There's a gas leak at—"

Lightning snaked from the sky with deadly purpose and struck one of the streetlights directly across from them. It blinded them but Sabelle heard the snap, the sizzle, the *boom* as the light exploded.

"Jesus," Ryan exclaimed, turning in to her as a fiery blast pressed against her eardrums, so loud it deafened.

"Get down!" He hauled her to the ground with him before she had the chance.

They hit the concrete hard, Ryan beneath her, cushioning her fall before rolling on top of her as a blistering wind seared them. Hot debris shattered windows and impaled the buildings lining both sides of the street. It sucked all of the oxygen away with a shriek. Sabelle screamed—or at least she thought she did. She couldn't hear her own cry over the destruction. It seemed to go on in never-ending waves and yet it was done in seconds, leaving ominous silence in its wake.

Ryan lifted his head and looked at her. "You all right?"

At least she thought that's what he said. She couldn't hear, but she nodded anyway, not really sure if it was true.

"Brandy," he called, already on his feet and pulling Sabelle up with him.

Brandy darted out of a doorway a few feet away, barking madly, wild-eyed.

"It's okay, it's okay," Ryan said, hunkering down so she could smell him. Apparently, the dog needed Ryan's scent as much as Sabelle did.

She stared at the sidewalk, taking short, quick breaths when she wanted one deep one. Her hands shook and her eyes streamed from the smoke. Terror poisoned her bloodstream and blanked her mind. Some distant part of her noticed that the hail had stopped. Was that a good or bad sign? She didn't know.

"Sabelle," Ryan said. She thought it might be the second time. He stepped in front of her and took her face in his warm hands. "You okay? Are you hurt?"

His gaze moved over her and he seemed to find his own answer. He drew her into his arms and gratefully she pressed her face to his throat as her body shook with reaction. He turned them both so he could see the damage to Love's.

Across the street a black cloud of smoke thundered out of the hole where the front doors of Love's used to be. The upstairs was a jagged silhouette outlined in fire. The flames stretched high and swept across the sky with glee.

It had happened. And, against all odds, she'd succeeded. Ryan still lived. Because of her.

"Hey," Ryan said gently. "Look at me."

She hid her fear as she met his gaze. He searched her eyes before murmuring, "Good girl."

Just like he said to the dog. She laughed, pressing her face back into his warmth.

Fire spread from Love's to engulf everything in front of it, turning the banners into sparking bursts of blue flame, and burning through the trees. Two doors down from the decimated pub, another explosion blew out windows and shot sizzling fingers into the sky where the wind snatched them up and whisked them along.

Without a word, she and Ryan ran away from it. Black smoke thundered after them and more flames jumped from awning to awning. Another explosion rattled windows and jarred the sidewalk. Sparks bounced in the sucking wind and a rain of embers showered her back. She looked over her shoulder to make sure she wasn't on fire and gave a sigh of relief when she didn't see anything smoldering. Brandy ran beside Ryan, head swiveling as she watched for danger.

Sabelle pulled her shirt over her mouth and nose to block out the suffocating smoke, but it stung her eyes and burned her throat. She coughed as it seared her lungs.

Dread made it hard to think. Hard to do anything but hold on while the fire licked its blazing tongue at everything it passed. She clenched her eyes tight, but *not* seeing made it worse.

Ryan turned down an alley that dead-ended at a concrete wall. She could see it ahead, pale blocks that reflected the smoke and fire barreling down on them. He raced toward it with purpose, pulling her along with him.

Sabelle chanced a glance over her shoulder. The smoke bore down on them and it seemed that something moved beneath the surface. It pressed out, stretching like a membrane. Then it was gone, leaving her with the impression of an eyeless face and gnashing teeth.

Once he reached the wall, Ryan braced his back against it and held out his hands for her. "Over the wall, Sabelle. That's it. Climb. Go."

She quickly stepped onto his thigh and he used his hands to lift as she shifted, hefting her weight until her right foot found his solid shoulder and her left swung over. She scraped her bare thighs as she straddled the sharp edge of cinder block.

Ryan scooped Brandy into his arms. She clung to him like a baby. Sabelle reached down and grabbed hold of Brandy's scruff as Ryan heaved her into Sabelle's arms.

"Watch out for cactus on the other side," he warned, as he swung up beside her. The fire surged to fill the space he'd just vacated and the building on the corner detonated, sending shrapnel everywhere. She felt the bite of its heat against her cheek, smelled burning hair, roasting flesh. Brandy yelped in pain.

"Go!" Ryan shouted.

She didn't have time to brace or consider. She wrapped her arms around the frightened dog and jumped.

A soft grassy bed waited on the other side, but she and Brandy came at it fast and flailing. Claws dug into Sabelle's side as the dog pushed off. Brandy spun and got her paws under her, but Sabelle slammed down on her shoulder and rolled.

Her head struck something hard and blinding pain ripped through her. She ended on her back, staring up at the startling sky. Ryan hit the ground with more skill but less bounce. She felt the impact of his body crash down. Somewhere in the distance she heard the scream of sirens racing toward them.

Ryan sat up quickly, shook his head to clear it, and looked around to find her. He rolled to his knees and crawled to where she lay, collapsing in the soft winter grass and pulling her up against him. A sharp whistle brought Brandy to his other side. Ryan put an arm around each and held them tight.

They were both breathing heavily, coughing as the smoke they'd inhaled caught in their chests. The fire didn't cross the wall, but the smoke followed them and blotted out the stars. It felt like a message—a show of power. Ryan's hand was warm and comforting against the bare skin at the small of her back. She concentrated on that instead.

They lay like that for a long moment, neither of them saying a word. Finally Ryan turned his head and looked at her.

He had questions and it wouldn't be long before he wanted answers. Sabelle gathered up her scattered wits, ticked off the salient points of her story in her mind, and tried not to get ahead of herself.

Step one, save Ryan Love. Mission accomplished.

Step two, bind him to her. Work in progress.

CHAPTER THREE

THE WALL THEY'D jumped had put them inside the grounds of a resort known for its prime location in downtown Tempe and for its picturesque setting. Even at this hour, lights still glowed brightly around the hotel, and as Ryan stepped from the grassy knoll where he'd landed with Sabelle, he felt like he'd stumbled onto a spotlit stage. Straight ahead, wide glass doors led from the lobby to a horseshoe driveway. This late, there weren't any cars waiting for the bellboys to unload them, but a handful of uniformed employees joined a few other people milling around, peering curiously down the street where the red and blue glow of emergency lights flashed. No one even noticed the two of them crossing the lawn to the street.

Things weren't exploding anymore, and the rain had helped with the spread of fire, but the smoke was thick and acrid. Brandy huddled close as Ryan led Sabelle around the corner and back to the place they'd fled. Neither one of them spoke. Oh, he had a list of questions a mile long for Miss Sabelle Whoever-She-Was, but right now he needed to see the damage to Love's, needed to know if it was as catastrophic as it seemed in that last glance before they'd fled. The storm eased by the moment, leaving a cold drizzle and damp gusts behind.

Drawn by the explosions and sirens, people had already started to gather at the edges of the disaster zone. Police tape gave them clear boundaries, but news and camera crews pushed up against it, wanting to capture any grisly detail they could. The businesses that had bordered Love's were in ruins as well as two across the street. Ryan's second-story loft had been incinerated—just as the woman beside him had predicted—and all but the shell of walls had been blasted away. Ash drifted in the air like dirty snowflakes and the char of his burned future made each breath bitter.

"Brandy," he said as they approached the gathering. "Look small."

Brandy dutifully hung her head and bent her doggy elbows—a trick he'd taught her years ago. She'd never look harmless, but she pulled off pitiful like a champ.

"Good girl."

Her tail wagged nervously.

Ryan was a big man, used to having people get out of his way. But he must have looked every bit as bad as he felt, because he heard murmurs and dismayed exclamations as the small crowd parted for them. When they reached the edge of the police tape, he glanced at Sabelle and caught her wincing.

"You okay?" he asked.

She nodded and reached for his hand, sucking in a soft breath at his touch. Every time they touched, as a matter of fact. As if some sensory overload were going on inside her. God knew she was blowing all his fuses.

He caught the attention of one of the uniformed officers and the man hurried over.

"Sir? Are you okay?" he asked, his worried gaze shifting between Ryan and Sabelle.

Ryan had to clear his throat a couple of times before he could speak. "I own Love's," he said. "We made it out just in time."

Suddenly cameras swung his way and he heard the inevitable babble coming from the news crews. They were torn between asking questions about his sister Roxanne and the explosions that had destroyed his family's pub. The officer motioned him through their barriers and over to a group of officials, saving him from the media's shark-infested waters.

Woodenly, Ryan told the officers what he knew. He'd smelled gas. He'd called 911, but everything started exploding before he could report the issue. They'd run for their lives.

"We've had reports of gas leakages all over Tempe," a tired, scruffy civilian with an official-looking badge around his neck told them. Ryan guessed that he worked for the gas and electric company. "All at the same time. Never seen anything like it. We're lucky that it happened so late. No serious injuries or deaths so far."

Lucky.

Warring emotions gripped Ryan. Thankfulness, that no one else had suffered. Relief, that there was an explanation for the destruction that only involved faulty gas lines. And anger, because once again Ryan was left to pick up pieces that he had no hope of ever reassembling. His family had been through so much—too much. He couldn't see a way out of this.

His vision blurred and he lowered his head, rubbing his stinging eyes. Hearing Sabelle in his mind telling him she'd come to warn him.

Come from where? How? *Why?*

Beside him, Sabelle's soft touch on his arm tried to offer comfort but only managed to churn his confusion into something worse.

A polite officer with thin blond hair and a square jaw ushered them to an emergency vehicle where two young female EMTs rinsed their eyes, gave them water and blankets, and treated the worst of their injuries until the officer they'd spoken to earlier appeared again.

"Just a couple of questions, Mr. Love," he said. "Any chance you made it out with your ID?"

Ryan had stuffed his wallet in the pack with his money and clothes. Now he carefully pulled it out, knowing that if the officer caught a glimpse of the money stashed in the bottom beneath his clothes, the routine questions wouldn't be so routine anymore. There was no way he'd be able to explain why he'd run from his bar just in the nick of time, yet managed to grab his money.

"Do you have ID, ma'am?" the polite officer asked.

The desperate gleam in Sabelle's eyes spurred Ryan to speak before he thought. "Her purse was upstairs," he said smoothly. "There wasn't time to get it."

"But you had time to pack?" asked an officer Ryan hadn't noticed. The man stepped into the light and settled a look on the two of them that he probably practiced in front of a mirror. He had dark curly hair and black eyes. Ryan almost smiled. Reece would have called the pair Starsky and Hutch. Ryan could still hear Reece's laughter in his head.

It felt like a lifetime ago.

"We were packing for a little getaway," Ryan said to the cop who looked like Starsky. "I brought the backpack down first. Sabelle was still in the loft getting dressed when I smelled the gas."

He impressed himself with the smooth cadence of the lie at the same time he wondered at the insanity of telling it. But covering for Sabelle seemed less involved than explaining how he'd found her bare naked in the parking lot a few minutes before she'd warned him he was going to die.

Starsky focused on Sabelle and her vagabond outfit. "That's you? You're Sybil?"

"Sabelle," she corrected with a sweet smile.

The officer waited for the rest of it. When Sabelle grew silent, he prompted, "Last name?"

She hid her anxiety well, but all of them caught the desperate glance she gave Ryan.

Ash still sifted down around them and the cold plumed her breath. Ryan forced himself to stay quiet and let her do her own digging. He already felt like he was in too deep.

ERIN QUINN

It didn't take her long. "Snow," she replied. "Sabelle Snow."

Ryan gave a mental groan as Starsky's head came up, his gaze filled with suspicion. Sabelle blinked those guileless eyes at him and finally the officer nodded, and wrote *Snow* on his tablet. Reservation glittered in his eyes, but Ryan and Sabelle weren't suspects. They were victims and he had no real reason to question them.

"Address?"

This was the time to cut the tie. To distance himself from Sabelle while he still had the chance. But she'd saved his life. Brandy's, too.

"You're looking at it," Ryan said, taking her hand and pulling her close as he pointed to the disaster zone he used to call home.

Sabelle gave him a furtive, grateful glance. Starsky's gaze moved from the tangle of her hair, over her pretty, dirty face, and down her ample curves in a quick sweep.

"We're lucky to be alive," Ryan said, cutting off any further questions, his voice unsteady enough to bring the point home. "We took what we had in our hands."

"More than lucky," Hutch agreed, staring at the destruction all around them.

"You Loves get lucky a lot," Starsky said, brows raised. "Some of you, four, five times."

Starsky's reference to Ryan's brother and sister and the inexplicable, *miraculous* way the twins had cheated death in the past felt like a jab with a sharp point into a

30

place that was already raw. Reece wasn't cheating death anymore and Roxanne had gone into hiding to avoid the relentless media. It was nothing to joke about.

"That's a good one, Officer," Ryan mocked. "You should tell that at parties."

To keep reading, buy
The Three Fates of Ryan Love
(Book 2 in the Beyond Series)
from your favorite bookseller.

For a complete book list of Erin Quinn's titles, go to
http://www.erinquinnbooks.com/Books.htm

www.ingramcontent.com/pod-product-compliance
Lightning Source LLC
Chambersburg PA
CBHW060425130626
46555CB00005B/2215

* 9 7 8 0 9 9 0 8 8 7 6 0 7 *